Safe Guard

By Amy Reece

Safe Guard

Copyright © 2017 by Amy Reece.
All rights reserved.
First Print Edition: August 2017

Limitless Publishing, LLC
Kailua, HI 96734
www.limitlesspublishing.com

Formatting: Limitless Publishing

ISBN-13: 978-1-64034-200-2
ISBN-10: 1-64034-200-1

Dedication

This is for the women who do it all: marriage, career, and family. Keep kickin' ass and takin' names, ladies! We rock!

Chapter One

Hugh

October

I'm going to kill my sister. It was his first thought as Chrissy walked up the aisle toward Finn and his groomsmen. His second was more along the lines of: *I am in so much trouble.* He'd done a decent job of denying his attraction for his brother's partner for the past few months, but how could he ignore the vision gliding toward him? He was used to seeing her in her work clothes and that was fine by him. It was easier to think of her as only a friend when she was wearing her usual jeans and blazer, although those tight jeans had fueled quite a few uncomfortably sexy dreams lately. God, he wouldn't get any sleep tonight!

He knew one of his sisters, probably both, were responsible for choosing the bridesmaids' dresses. Mel may have had some voice in her own wedding, but he knew beyond a shadow of a doubt Cara and

1

Izzy were to blame for the midnight blue strapless creation all three of them were wearing. He caught a glimpse of both of his sisters advancing up the aisle behind Chrissy, but they couldn't hold his attention. His eyes were glued to her golden tan, sculpted shoulders, and arms. He'd known, could tell, she was incredibly fit and strong, but seeing her in the flesh—God, so much flesh!—was another thing entirely. The bodice of the dress lovingly encased two firm, perfectly sized breasts, which he knew would haunt his dreams for months. The skirt was short, of course, highlighting her endless slender legs. She must be nearly six feet tall. He'd stood next to her often enough to know she was just a few inches shorter than his own six foot three inches. He dragged his gaze back to her gorgeous face. She'd done something different, fancier with her short blonde hair. It was slicked back behind her ears with a sparkly clip on one side. He'd always preferred women with long hair, but the short, sexy cut suited her.

She reached the front of the aisle and glanced at him briefly, flashing him a quick, hesitant smile before she moved to her place. Mel had asked her to be a bridesmaid to fill out her side since Finn had three brothers and wanted them all to stand up with him. Izzy and Cara were her other bridesmaids, and the four women had become close over the past two months since Finn and Mel had announced their engagement. Because he was Finn's best man, he'd spent quite a bit of time with her as well as they planned the various wedding-related activities. It was heaven. It was torture.

Cara, the maid of honor, finally reached the front and took her place right before the music changed and Mel appeared at the end of the aisle. Oh, wow. She was achingly beautiful and only had eyes for his brother. Hugh glanced at his brother and was struck by the expression of utter love and contentment on his face. *What would it be like to feel that way about a woman? I'm starting to think I'll never know.* He was thirty-four and hadn't managed to find the right one yet. He'd thought the last one was *the one*, but no. Definitely not.

He fumbled a bit when it came time to hand the ring over to Finn. He'd been staring at Chrissy, of course. He couldn't begin to remember what the homily had been about or if there even was one. Surely there had been. He barely remembered taking communion. "Here. Sorry."

Finn gave him a quick glance and frown, but turned back to his bride without comment. Within a very few minutes, Father Ortega was declaring Finn and Mel man and wife and his brother was kissing his bride. He was happy for them; they both deserved nothing but happiness after what they'd been through in the past few months. First, Finn had been hit by a car while out running, nearly killing him. Hugh still got a pang in his gut when he remembered Finn lying in a hospital bed in ICU, hooked up to more machines than he could count. Finn had finally gotten rid of his walking boot two weeks before. He'd attacked his physical therapy with steely determination; he vowed he would be walking, unaided, for his wedding. He made it, but still had a noticeable limp.

Mel had been stalked for several months, nearly losing her life when her house was set ablaze. Hugh had recently finished the reconstruction that added a second floor above the new two-car garage as well as a gorgeous gourmet kitchen. Mel loved to cook and it hadn't taken much to talk her into it. He'd given her a great price, of course, basically doing all the work for the cost of the materials. He'd paid for the labor for his crew out of his own pocket, quietly telling Finn to consider it a wedding present. He hadn't wanted to make a profit from his future sister-in-law. She and Finn had decided to sell his house and move into hers, a wise decision as far as Hugh was concerned.

He watched the newly married couple kiss, smiling as it went on longer than usual. He heard Seamus and Tony whistle and whoop and saw Finn and Mel exchange a private grin as they finally broke apart. Then they were recessing and Hugh took Cara's arm to lead her to the limousine, which would take them back to his parents' house, where the reception was to be held. They had a lengthy stop for photographs to endure first, however. They finally arrived at his parents' house and had more wedding ritual to observe before they were finally allowed to eat. He then proceeded to pretend not to watch Chrissy during the delicious sit down dinner his mother had had catered. Mel had wanted a small backyard wedding and allowed Finn's mother, Moira, to have her way if it stayed within the limits Finn had set: twenty-five guests in addition to their immediate family. Hugh looked around and narrowed his eyes as he realized his mother's math was somewhat questionable. If there were fewer than a hundred people here, he'd be surprised. Mel had graciously accepted the need for the ceremony to be in the church, as the DeLucas were devout Catholics.

"Holy shit! Did you have any idea Chris had all that going on?" Tony flipped a rented white chair around and straddled it. He'd removed his midnight blue bow tie hours before, along with his jacket, and looked much more casual now with his sleeves rolled up and shirt untucked.

Hugh tamped down the instant ire he felt when his brother mentioned her. He raised his beer and took a long swig to give himself time to respond evenly. "Hadn't noticed." He feared saying anything else, knowing his brother would gleefully use it against him. He'd worked too hard to hide his latent attraction for Chrissy over the past few months to give it up so easily to his younger brother.

"Well, look at her! She's hot! How old do you think she is? She seems older, don't you think?"

"She's thirty-two. Too old for you." He winced, wishing he could take the words back. They'd slipped out before he'd even thought about it.

Tony paused, beer mid-way to his lips, an unholy grin spreading across his handsome face. He glanced at his brother before taking a long pull from the beer and setting it on the table. "Well, I'll let her be the judge of that. She's one of the few women here I'm not related to, so I'm going to ask her to dance. We'll see where it goes from there. Who knows? Maybe I'll get lucky. She might be into

5

younger men."

Hugh gripped his bottle hard and gritted his teeth, determined not to strangle his brother in the middle of Finn's wedding reception. "Yeah, well, good luck with that." He shrugged as if it meant nothing to him that his little brother was going to hit on the gorgeous woman he'd been trying not to obsess about for months. He couldn't afford to get involved with another woman who valued her career over and above everything else in her life. His heart simply couldn't take it.

Tony grinned again—damn him—and stood. "Don't wait up, Hugh."

Hugh watched through narrowed eyes as he crossed the yard and approached Chrissy. He'd hoped to see her smile and shake her head, but although she smiled, it was more radiant than apologetic. Then she placed her hand in Tony's and allowed him to lead her to the crowded dance floor. Hugh swallowed the bile rising in his throat and realized his beer was empty. He went to get another from the bar, although he didn't want it; anything was better than watching his brother dance with her. But once he had a fresh beer he couldn't keep his eyes from straying to the dance floor. She was a good dancer. Tony was enthusiastic, and it was making Chrissy laugh. Hugh had never seen her so carefree and found himself enchanted; at the same time, he was dying inside. The music changed to a slower song and Tony held his arms out. *Step away, Chrissy. Shake your pretty head at him and walk the hell away.* She smiled and stepped into his arms. He watched as Tony slid an arm around her waist, then let it drift lower. *Shit. Enough is enough!* He set his beer on the table rather abruptly and crossed the yard, coming to a halt next to them.

"Get lost, Tony. This dance is mine." He knew he sounded like an ass, but it was better than punching his brother in the face.

***

Chris

How dare he? He waits all night to ask me to dance, then butts in like a goddamn Neanderthal? Tony was no help. He laughed and handed her over to Hugh as if she were some helpless female, as if she had no choice in the matter. Well, she'd show them! She opened her mouth, prepared to deliver a blistering set-down to both brothers, but Hugh took her hand at that moment. They'd never touched before. All words—in fact, the power of speech itself—abandoned her. His hand was rough and warm, sending a physical jolt up her arm to blitz her brain into stupidity and compliance. He slid his other arm around her waist and pulled her in close. She raised her other hand and set it on his broad shoulder and let him lead her into the slow dance. *God, he smells so good. It should be illegal to smell this amazing.* She'd noticed before, but she'd never had such an intimate dose. She had no idea what aftershave he used, but the way it mixed with his detergent and his own particular scent was heady. She stumbled slightly and he pulled her even closer.

"I've got you," he whispered against her hair.

7

She swallowed, sudden tears unaccountably close to the surface. *What the hell? Why does this man affect me so?* She'd just recently managed to learn to control her clumsiness around him. When they'd first met, she couldn't be around him without tripping over something—often her own two feet—or dropping whatever she happened to be holding. It was ridiculous and embarrassing. She was no inexperienced ingénue, after all. She'd built a successful career in a male-dominated field, making detective before her thirtieth birthday, a record in her precinct—male or female—until Finn came along and bumped up against it. But whenever she found herself near Hugh DeLuca, she lost her freaking mind. He seemed completely oblivious and uninterested in her, however, as evidenced by the way he had refused to ask her to dance all evening. She knew it would be better for her fragile self-esteem if she stayed away. *Maybe later.* Right now, it felt too good to be held against his warm, solid body. It had been so long since anyone had held her. He was tall enough to make her feel less like the Amazon she resembled and she decided to enjoy it for the brief dance. What harm could it do?

Tony had been fun to dance with, but she felt no attraction to him, although he was certainly good-looking—all the DeLuca boys were—and a lot of fun. She'd danced with Seamus and Finn earlier, but Hugh hadn't asked her. He'd watched her—she couldn't miss his brooding glare—but he never asked her to dance. She'd even danced with his father, for heaven's sake! She'd been tempted to march across the yard and demand to know what the hell was wrong with him, but hadn't wanted to cause a scene at Finn's wedding.

"Why?" She hadn't meant to say the word aloud.

"Why what?" His words vibrated against her body.

She lifted her head and considered his achingly handsome face. "Why did it take you so long to ask me to dance? Every single one of your male relatives asked me, but it took you until 10:30 to ask me, or barge in, rather."

He sighed. "I'm sorry, Chrissy. I don't have a good excuse."

She'd been itching for a fight, but he took the wind out of her sails with his apology. She narrowed her eyes at him, then simply nodded and rested her head against his shoulder. He pulled her even closer.

"You look beautiful tonight. I wish I'd told you earlier."

So did she; she'd felt conspicuous and too exposed all evening. She'd cringed when Cara and Izzy had insisted on the strapless dresses for Mel's wedding. They both looked amazing, of course, with their dark hair and perfect, petite bodies. She'd never worn anything so revealing. There was so much more of her to hang out of this dress—yards of arms and legs, it felt like. She'd always struggled to feel confident in her own body—all five foot eleven inches of it—and had been mostly successful, working hard to keep toned and fit. But a tight, strapless dress was another matter entirely. Hugh's compliment felt nice, even if it was a bit late.

She knew why she was so nervous around him, of course. It wasn't as if it was any big mystery. Her ridiculous crush on him had come on so suddenly. Six months ago, she'd rushed to the hospital as soon as she heard about Finn's accident, and Hugh was the first member of his family she met. She'd been caught unaware by his rugged good looks. He'd introduced himself and she'd responded by blurting her name—she hadn't gone by *Chrissy* since college. She'd been strictly *Chris* since her police academy days. But Hugh had called her Chrissy ever since. She privately loved it, hugging it to herself like a sweet secret. *Stupid, stupid, stupid!* She felt his thumb absently caressing the skin of her back and swallowed hard. It felt incredible.

Their bodies swayed together for another minute or two until the music ended. Did he press a kiss against her hair? No, of course not. Why on earth would he do that? *Wishful thinking, girl!*

"Thanks for the dance, Chrissy."

"I don't suppose I could talk you into buying me a beer, could I?" Where had those words come from? She'd intended to tell him he was welcome and leave him standing on the dance floor, hopefully feeling awkward.

He said nothing, but smiled and ushered her off the floor toward the bar.

Two beers later—it was an open bar so she didn't feel too bad—she was feeling the effects of the liquid courage and could enjoy laughing with him, sharing anecdotes from their respective jobs. He made construction work sound interesting. Or maybe it was simply that she loved anything he said with his deep voice. God, she was pathetic.

"So, you're staying at the house while they're on their honeymoon?" Hugh gestured to the newlyweds as he took a sip of his beer and set it on the table.

"Yeah. It will be better for CJ and Fluff to stay in their own house rather than be boarded. That's always hard on pets."

"That's really nice of you. Finn said you refused to let them pay you for housesitting."

"He's my partner and Mel's my friend. You don't take money from friends. Besides, I don't have any pets or plants, so it's no problem." It wasn't a burden to give up her crappy little apartment for two weeks to stay in Mel and Finn's beautiful home while they were in Hawaii.

"If you need anything while you're there, give me a call. Okay? You have my number, right?"

She nodded. She wouldn't need anything, of course. She was perfectly capable of dealing with anything that might come up. She carried a gun, after all. She wished she had the nerve to tell him to stop by if he had a free moment, but she'd used up all her courage when she'd basically forced him to buy her a beer. He'd have to make the next move if there was going to be a next move. Did she want that? *Stupid question.* Of course she wanted that. She'd been crushing on him like a high school girl for months, stopping short of doodling his name in her notebook. It wasn't like her. Or maybe it was. She'd never been very good at letting men know she was interested, and since she and her long-time boyfriend, Greg, had called it quits two years ago, there had been nothing but the most casual of dates.

"Chrissy?" He was staring at her, eyebrows raised.

Crap. She'd been so busy obsessing about him she missed his question. She felt herself flushing as she ducked her head. "Sorry. What was the question?"

His crooked smile caused her stomach to twist. "Dance with me? They're playing another slow one."

She answered with a crooked smile of her own and nodded. It might be stupid, but she'd take what he offered.

They didn't speak during the dance, the final one of the evening. Mel and Finn had slipped away sometime earlier and the guests now began drifting away. She would spend tonight at her own apartment and move to their house the next morning, once they left for Kauai.

"Let me walk you to your car."

"That's not necessary, Hugh, but thanks. I am a cop, you know. I can take care of myself."

"I know you can." He followed her to the table where she'd left her purse. "But I'd be surprised if you have your gun stashed in that tiny purse. Besides, maybe I'm the one who needs your protection."

She grinned at him and realized she'd enjoyed the last hour. When she managed to let go of her nerves, she was pleased to remember she had a personality buried not too far under the surface. He was fun to talk to and had a great sense of humor. She'd laughed more with him in the last hour or so than she had in quite a while. *Crap. I'm in so much trouble.*

Chapter Two

Hugh

Three days. That's how long he managed to stay away from her. *Pathetic.* Yet here he was, parking his truck in front of his brother's house after a long day at work. He didn't even know if she was home. He grabbed the six-pack he'd stopped to pick up and called to his dog. "Let's go, Bob. Maybe she'll think you're cute enough to let us in."

She wasn't home. He could hear Fluff barking as the doorbell rang, but she didn't answer. A quick check of the garage showed him her car was there, parked alongside Finn's Jeep. He knew Izzy had driven Finn and Mel to the airport in Mel's new Honda CR-V, and then had taken it back to her place to make room for Chrissy's car. A slight twinge of worry hit, but he told himself she was probably out for a walk or something. He made himself at home on the front porch and twisted the top off one of the beers. He was halfway through it when he realized she was most likely out on a date, and the guy had picked her up. *Fine. Maybe I'll just sit here until she gets home so I can check this guy out. There won't be any goodnight kisses on the front porch if I'm here.* He felt extremely satisfied with his plan as he took another long pull from his beer. But the thought of her out with some other guy ruined the taste.

Fifteen minutes later he saw her round the far corner at a run, then slow down to a walk, hands on her hips, breathing heavily. She didn't see him until she turned up the walk to the house. His heart soared as he realized she wasn't out with someone else.

"Hey, Chrissy." He lost the battle to keep his eyes off her long legs. He could see even more of them in her tiny running shorts than he had in the dress the other night.

"Uh, hey, Hugh. Don't you have a key?" She removed her earbuds and flopped down on the front step, leaning back on her elbows.

He watched the sweat trickle down the side of her face. Sweat shouldn't be sexy, but it was on her. He imagined licking it off, then firmly shut that line of thought down. "Of course, but only for emergencies. I would never disrespect your privacy by using it while you're here."

"But you bust in on Finn and Mel whenever you please?"

"God, no. More than half the time I'd probably catch them doing stuff I don't want to see. I'll leave that to Cara." He twisted the top off a beer and handed it to her.

"Thanks." She tilted her head back and chugged.

"Mmm. Why have I been bothering with water after a run? Beer is so much better." She grinned at him. "And who is this?"

"That's Bob." The Golden Retriever had cozied up next to her and took a swipe with his long tongue at her salty neck. Hugh desperately wanted to take his place.

"Bob?" She laughed and playfully pushed the dog away. He came back for more and she soon had him on his back while she rubbed his belly.

"Yeah. I guess I'm not very creative when it comes to naming pets." He stared as she played with his dog, unsure what to say or even why he was there.

"Do you want to come in? He won't eat Fluff, will he?"

"Nah. Bob and Fluff are great friends. CJ doesn't love him, but she ignores him, for the most part. I'd love to come in." He gathered the beer and followed her inside. Fluff met them and pranced crazily around their feet. When he saw Bob, however, the humans were forgotten. The dogs trotted off, Bob squeezing himself through the smallish dog door to follow Fluff outside.

Chrissy grabbed a glass from the cabinet, treating Hugh to a tiny glimpse of her stomach as she reached. "You want some water?"

He shook his head. "Have you eaten yet?"

She smiled and shook her head while she drank the water. "I don't think I have much here."

"You want to order a pizza?" He held his breath as he waited for her answer.

"Hmm. How do you feel about Thai food?"

"Passionately."

She chuckled. "Is that passionately positive or negative?"

"Definitely positive. The spicier the better. We could bring it back here. The backyard is gorgeous. I should know since I drew up the plans for it."

"I'll call in our order. Any chance you'd go pick it up while I grab a quick shower?"

He readily agreed, grateful she seemed to want to spend more time with him. The thought of her in the shower made him grab another beer while she phoned in their order. Forty minutes later, he let himself back in, juggling the bag of food and the bottle of chilled white wine he'd stopped for. Yes, he was trying to impress her. He didn't want to stop to examine the reasons too closely, however.

She was on the back patio, setting out plates and napkins on the glass-topped wrought iron table. She'd changed into a short, sleeveless dress and her hair was still damp. "Ooh, wine. I'll grab some glasses. Did you get chopsticks?"

"Of course. You look pretty." God, had that sounded as clumsy as it felt?

She paused, her hand on the back door. "Thanks."

He shook his head at his own stupidity as he plated the food. She returned with the wine glasses and a corkscrew and set about opening the wine and pouring them each a glass.

"Cheers." She raised her glass.

"Sláinte." He raised his own glass and touched it to hers.

"What does that mean? I've heard you say it

before. Finn says it too."

"It's Irish for 'good health.' Our mother's influence." He took a sip of the Sauvignon Blanc he'd chosen to go with the Thai food.

"You have such an interesting family." She sipped her own wine, then picked up her chopsticks and expertly used them to lift a chunk of green curry tofu to her mouth.

He was momentarily distracted by her pink tongue sneaking out to lick a stray bit of sauce from her lips. He cleared his throat and took a bite of his own red curry chicken. "You mean the whole Irish/Italian nightmare?" His mother had grown up in Belfast and met his father, a second-generation Italian immigrant, when she came to the United States for an exchange program. They'd taken turns naming their children, which explained why they had Hugh, Isabella, Finn, Cara, Seamus, and Antonio.

"Oh, I don't know about 'nightmare.' It seems like you all get along pretty well."

"We do, for the most part. I'm closest with Finn and Izzy. I'm so much older than the others I don't always understand what they're into."

"You're only thirty-four, Hugh. Hardly an old man."

So, she had gone to the trouble of finding out his age? Interesting. "Sometimes it feels like it. Are you a vegetarian?" He waved his chopsticks at her tofu.

"No. I just like tofu."

"Really? I thought it was something vegetarians only put up with since they can't have meat. I've heard it's disgusting."

"How have you reached the ripe old age of thirty-four and never tasted tofu? Here." She picked up a chunk with her chopsticks and held it out toward him.

He raised his eyebrows, but leaned forward and took the bite from her.

"So? What do you think?"

"It's chewy."

She gave him an unimpressed look.

"But not terrible. It's pretty innocuous, actually. It really soaks up the sauce, which is delicious. I've never tried the green curry. I always order red."

She smiled. "Yeah. That's why I like it. Do you mind?" She motioned with her chopsticks toward his plate.

He loved the idea of sharing food with her. It seemed so intimate, something a couple would do. "Help yourself."

She chewed thoughtfully. "That's really spicy. I like it."

So, they ended up sharing from each other's plates. They finished and were drinking the last of the wine, watching the gorgeous New Mexico sunset. He liked that neither seemed to feel the need to fill the occasional silence with inane chatter. It felt comfortable sitting here with her, and he realized that while he desired her as a woman— definitely, and in a bad way—he enjoyed her as a friend. He knew it would be better for his heart and peace of mind if they remained the latter.

"What about your family, Chrissy? Did you grow up here?"

"No. I grew up in El Paso. My parents and my

younger sister still live there. I came here for college and never left. I love Albuquerque. It's not nearly as hot as El Paso."

"True. Do you visit often?"

"Not often enough, according to my mother." She flashed him a wry grin. "They're planning a visit here soon. They usually come up for Balloon Fiesta."

"Are they staying with you?"

"No, thank God. I only have a one bedroom apartment. They always stay at a bed and breakfast in the South Valley."

They sat for another few minutes before her cell phone buzzed. "Aww, dammit. I knew this was too good to be true." She grabbed it, checked the number, and answered. "Yeah. This is Hart." She listened for a few moments. "Okay. Send me the address. I'll be there in fifteen." She clicked off and let the phone drop to her lap as she leaned her head against the back of her seat. "Fucking criminals," she muttered. "They have no respect for my time off."

"You have to go in to work?"

She nodded without looking at him. "Double homicide. Shit." She heaved herself out of her chair and reached for their plates.

Hugh took the plates from her. "I'll clear this up. You go on. I'll lock up when I'm done."

She put her hands on her hips and laughed ruefully. "That would actually be great. Thanks, Hugh. I need to change."

When she reappeared a few minutes later, she had changed into jeans and a button-up shirt with her shoulder holster and service weapon. She grabbed a navy blazer, put one arm in, and struggled to find the other. He saw her badge hanging on a chain around her neck.

Hugh set the dish towel aside and stepped behind her to help. "Here." He settled the jacket on her shoulders and turned her to face him. "Be careful, okay?" He gave her a long look that said much more than his words had. *Be safe. I care, more than I have any right to, but there it is.*

"I always am." She looked into his eyes. *Thank you for caring. It's nice to have someone at home who does.*

He cleared his throat and they awkwardly stepped away from each other, the momentary connection broken.

"I've got to go."

"Yeah. I'll lock up." He finished cleaning up their dishes, then spent a few minutes checking the timers and bubblers in the yard and plants outside, the batteries in the smoke detectors, and the locks on the new windows. He gave Fluff and CJ fresh water and a small treat each. When he could find nothing else to check, he found a piece of note paper in a downstairs desk drawer and scrawled a note.

Chrissy,

Please send me a text when you get home, no matter what time.

Hugh

He propped it against the clock on the nightstand in the guest bedroom. "Come on, Bob. Time to go home." He locked his brother's house and followed the dog to his truck.

***

Chris

She pulled her car into an available spot and sighed. She'd been having such a nice time with Hugh and hated to leave so abruptly. You could have knocked her over with a feather when she started up the walkway and saw him sitting on the porch. She hadn't heard a word from him since the wedding and thought she must have imagined the connection they'd shared. Dancing with him had been amazing; the feel of his strong arms around her was something she could become addicted to. They'd laughed together and found so much to talk about after she'd suggested he buy her a beer. He'd joked about her being a cheap date since it was an open bar. She smiled as she remembered. He was definitely more serious than his brother. She supposed an outsider would consider him not quite as handsome as Finn, either. His hair was not quite as dark and his eyes were a lighter blue—almost icy—than Finn's startling cobalt eyes, but whereas she'd always realized Finn was extremely good-looking, she'd never been attracted to him, not even briefly. She could not say the same for Hugh. She'd been a blithering idiot from the second they met. Something about him woke feelings deep inside her, like a sucker punch to the gut. But she feared he didn't feel the same. But then why was he waiting on her porch? His mixed signals were making here head spin. Maybe she'd work up the courage and simply ask him about it. *Yeah, right.*

She forced herself out of the car and ducked under the yellow crime scene tape barring the path to the picnic area in the Foothills Open Space area. The Sandia mountains towered above the park, which was nestled at the foot of the range. One of the best things about living in Albuquerque was the proximity of this majestic mountain range. Chris often spent her weekends hiking the trails. This particular open space had been developed into a lovely park with paved paths and scenic stops, some containing stone picnic enclosures with tables and smooth concrete floors. The sun had set a half-hour or so before, but the nearly full moon provided enough light to navigate the narrow paved path. The rattlesnakes would all be sleeping at this time of night, so she had no worries about inadvertently stepping on one. She wrenched her gaze away from the rustic beauty of the surroundings and stepped into the stone enclosure. Portable lights had been set up to illuminate the scene. A photographer was clicking photos of the two bodies, one slumped across the picnic table, the other sprawled on the ground. Uniformed officers, a mixture of state and county, stood around talking and taking notes. "Hey, Dean. What have we got?" The coppery tang of blood mixed with the stench of vomit and shit filled the air. Not many people realized bodies often defecated shortly after death and at least one of these two had.

The photographer lowered his camera and stood straight. "Oh, hey, Chris. These two geniuses shot each other, judging by the look of things. Witness barfed in the corner."

"Oh, for fuck's sake! And they couldn't shoot each other in a city park so the local police would have to deal with it? They had to pick state land. I was on a date." It was a bit of an exaggeration, but it had felt like a date.

"Oh, really? Who's the lucky guy?" Dean was suddenly all ears.

Shit. Why couldn't I keep my mouth shut? She didn't want it spread around that she was lusting after her partner's brother, especially since her partner knew nothing about it. "Oh, just a guy. No one special." She leaned in for a closer look at the two victims, noting the head wound on the one slumped across the table. He'd been shot in the forehead and the back of his head was a bloody mess of hair, brain matter, and bone. Her green curry churned slightly in her stomach. She'd seen similar things on a regular basis over the last decade, but you never got totally immune to it. "Well, this guy died as soon as he was shot, so I'm guessing he fired first, unless there was someone else involved." She moved to examine the other victim. He was sprawled across the dusty floor of the picnic enclosure, a large pool of blood beneath him. She noted animal prints tracking through the blood, but it didn't appear as if the body had been chewed anywhere. Both victims were dressed in baggy blue jeans and t-shirts and had a plethora of visible tattoos. "This one is gut-shot. Looks like he bled out before he could get very far. I'm guessing this was a drug deal gone bad. Check their pockets for cash and drugs. Where's the witness who called it in?"

"Next enclosure over." Dean waved vaguely to the left and continued to snap photos.

"Holler when the coroner gets here." Chris turned and trudged the fifty or so yards across an unpaved side path to the next enclosed picnic area. She could see how this out-of-the way nature trail would hold a lot of attraction for a sleazy drug deal; it was fairly remote, yet not far from the city, and the stone enclosures around the picnic tables offered privacy as well as a wind break. In the next one, a fifty-ish woman sat on the picnic bench facing outward, a leash clasped loosely in her hand. Her face under a short mop of salt-and-pepper hair was pale and chalky. The black and brown terrier at the end of the leash stood, tail wagging, as Chris approached. She squatted to pet the small dog. "Hello, ma'am." She stood and held out her hand to the woman. "I'm Detective Hart with the New Mexico State Police. Can I get your name, address, and telephone number?" She retrieved a small notebook and pen from her pocket and began jotting down the woman's information. Her name was Marilyn Davis and she lived about a mile away. "Can you tell me what happened here?"

"I was walking Byron," she gestured to the dog, "like I do every evening. He likes to chase rabbits and lizards along this path." She chuckled, then appeared horrified that she could laugh in such a situation.

"It's all right, ma'am." Chris knew the average person had no idea how to behave when confronted by sudden, violent death. "Just tell me what you saw."

"I didn't see anything at first. Byron was the one who found them." She shuddered. "I let him off his leash when we got here to the park. I know it says not to, but he's such a good dog. He always comes when I call."

"That's no problem." Chris couldn't care less about this woman breaking petty park rules. "So Byron found the bodies?"

Marilyn nodded. "I figured he'd found a dead rabbit, the way he was sniffing around. But then I walked around the corner and saw the b-bodies. He was walking through the blood."

Chris nodded; that explained the little paw prints tracking through the blood pool.

"I screamed and grabbed him up. I got blood all over my blouse." She gestured down her torso. "I hope it comes out." She started brushing her hands uselessly down her blouse.

Chris knew she wasn't going to get anything useful from the woman at the moment. "All right, Ms. Davis. I'm going to have the paramedics check you out and I'll talk to you again later, okay?"

The woman nodded, a blank expression on her face. Chris turned and walked away. She met the paramedics on the way.

"She may be going into shock," she said as she passed.

"We got it," one of them said.

She walked back to the first enclosure. "Have we got IDs on our two gang-bangers yet?"

A uniformed officer approached with a notebook. "Victim number one is Juan Esteban Chavez, twenty-three. Lengthy rap sheet and a known member of Los Locos. Victim number two is Javier David Gonzales, nineteen. Also a member of Los Locos and a slightly shorter rap sheet. We found what looks like methamphetamines on Gonzales and a lot of cash on Chavez."

Chris examined the bodies, working around the coroner, noting the neck tattoos and teardrop tattoos near the eyes on both victims. "You have a time of death?"

The coroner looked up from where he squatted beside the victim on the ground. "Liver temp says they died no more than four hours ago. I'll know more once I get them back to the morgue. Where's your partner? I heard he finally got back after his accident."

"Yeah, but he's on his honeymoon now. Hawaii."

"Lucky bastard. I'd kill to be in Hawaii right now." It was a mark of how inured they were to their given profession that neither winced at his remark. "So, you're pulling solo duty till he gets back? Sucks for you."

"It does indeed. Well, there's nothing else I can do here. Let me know when you finish the autopsies." She wrote another few notes, then closed her notebook and headed back to her car. She'd drive to the precinct, where she had a couple hours of reports to write. God, she hated days like this. She'd worked a full eight hours and now she was pulling another three to four.

Her report took even longer than it should have because her mind kept drifting back to her evening with Hugh. It had been exciting and comfortable at the same time. Where would it have led if she'd been able to stay? Maybe nowhere, but there was that moment right before she left. What was that about? She didn't know, but she was dying to find out, even if it was probably a terrible idea. She'd pretty much given up on finding a guy who was interested in the type of commitment she wanted. None of the guys she had dated, including her live-in boyfriend, Greg, had wanted a permanent commitment. It's what eventually ended what had been an otherwise good relationship. Other women managed to find a guy who wanted the whole marriage and family thing, so why was it so hard for her? She loved her career and had no intention of giving it up, but she was thirty-two and ready for more. Apparently more wasn't ready for her.

She finally arrived home around two a.m., exhausted and cranky. This evening had started out so much better than it ended. She only had enough energy to pull off her clothes and throw on the big, soft t-shirt she liked to wear to bed. She set her phone alarm and placed it on the nightstand. That's when she noticed the note. Her heart pounded as she read the words Hugh had scrawled. She grabbed her phone and sent her text.

Chris: Just got home and saw your note. I'm safe. I didn't even have to shoot anyone tonight.

28

Hugh: *Good to hear. Sleep well, Chrissy.*

She smiled and set her phone down. She was still smiling when she fell asleep.

Chapter Three

Hugh

He whistled as he walked into work. Bob followed, stopping to sniff under a hedge and began to dig. "Knock it off, buddy. Izzy will kill you if you dig up her flowers." The dog reluctantly gave up and ran to catch up, slipping in the door as Hugh held it open.

"Morning, Bob. Morning, Hugh. You seem chipper."

"Morning Malva. Is Izzy in yet?" The woman had been the receptionist at DeLuca Construction since Hugh was a teenager; he had no clue how old she was and was smart enough not to ask. He figured she'd announce her retirement one of these years. It was a bit unnerving to have someone working for you who had known you since you had acne and braces.

"Not yet."

"Okay. When she gets here, tell her I need to see her, please. Come on, Bob. Malva is not going to give you a piece of candy, no matter how hard you beg."

"Spoilsport," Malva muttered.

Hugh grinned and shut his office door after his dog followed him in. He checked email and voice mail for twenty minutes until his sister arrived, rushed and apologetic.

"I'm sorry, Hugh. Janey spilled her cereal and then threw a fit about having to change out of her My Little Pony shirt. What a morning!"

He smiled at the antics of his niece and rose to pour his flustered sister a cup of coffee. "Sit." He handed her the mug and backed her into the couch. "It's fine, Izzy. We don't watch clocks on each other."

"I know." She sighed and took a sip of the steaming, dark coffee. "I just want to carry my weight, you know?"

"Jesus, Izzy! You carry plenty of the weight around here." She took care of the financial part of the family business, handling it better than it ever had been, allowing them to expand and grow in ways never before possible. Her attention to detail allowed him to concentrate on what he did best: working with clients and making sure things went smoothly on job sites. They made a great team.

"Thanks, Hugh. It's just tough some days." She sipped her coffee again. Both were silent as they realized they were wading into deep conversational waters too early in the morning.

"So, how is the Kensington account coming?"

She seemed to appreciate the change of subject to something more work-oriented. "I've got the preliminary work done. I think we're ready to make a bid."

"Good. I'll make an appointment with the old man for later this week."

She sipped her coffee and stared at him over the rim of her mug.

"What?"

"Nothing." She smiled at him. "You seem to be in a good mood, that's all. You're not usually this talkative. Any particular reason?"

"Nope. It's a beautiful morning is all."

She studied him in that way she had; it had always made him squirm. She never said anything. She simply skewered him with her laser glare.

He stared back.

"Fine. I can take a hint." She rose and left his office, taking her coffee with her.

Hugh blew out a breath as the door closed behind her. He certainly didn't want to explain what was currently making him happy. His extremely nascent relationship with Chrissy was definitely not something he wanted to discuss with his sister. He wasn't ready to tip his hand quite yet. He worked for another hour, then gathered Bob and headed out to check a few job sites.

Things were going well at the site in the far Northeast Heights, where they were building a large custom home. Hugh noted the framing was nearly done and talked with the superintendent, Abe, about the possibility of beginning the exterior walls the next day. He checked the blueprints and did a thorough walk-through, part of his job he enjoyed the most. As much as possible, he left the office work to Izzy and spent his time talking with clients and making sure things ran smoothly in the field.

The next site, a housing development in Rio Rancho, was not going as well. As he crossed the Rio Grande river, he thought about the unpleasant conversation he was going to have with the superintendent on that site. It would be the last conversation with that particular superintendent unless he could get his job site running more efficiently in short order. When he pulled his truck into the area beside the office trailer, he noticed the general sloppiness of the site, something that didn't sit well with him. He entered the trailer without knocking and startled the man seated at a desk in the corner.

"Hey, Mark. What's up?" Hugh glanced around the office, noting the messiness extended here. He sighed, realizing the time had come. He crossed the room and seated himself in the metal folding chair placed near the desk. This close he could see the redness in the man's eyes and what looked like a sleep crease in his cheek. He'd heard plenty of rumors about the job superintendent's love of partying and probable alcoholism. "Everything going well here?"

"Uh, yeah. Sure. Why? Did somebody say something?" Mark was already on the defensive.

Hugh hated this part of the job. "You're behind schedule."

"I can't control the weather, Hugh. That rain has slowed everyone down."

Seriously? This guy was going to use rain as an excuse? In Albuquerque, where the annual total was less than nine inches, usually far less? Enough. "Okay, Mark. Pack your stuff. I want you off this job site in twenty minutes."

General cursing and blustering followed, as it usually did in situations like this. Hugh simply sat, waiting until the other man wore himself out.

"What am I gonna do, Hugh? I need a job."

"You had one, Mark...a good one. It seems to me you like partying more than you like working. You're down to fifteen minutes."

"You're a cold son of a bitch, you know that?" Mark stood and began yanking open desk drawers, piling his personal belongings on the top of the desk.

"Yeah, I know. I'll make sure Izzy has your check ready by the time you get back to the office." He left the trailer and went to find the foreman. He found him, along with the crew, smoking and chatting beside one of the company trucks. "Jacko! Come here a minute."

The bandy-legged foreman flicked his cigarette stump away and jogged over. "Hey, Boss. What do you want us to do? The super hasn't told us anything for, like, two days."

"Well, he's not the super of this job anymore. I'll send a new one out later this afternoon. For now, can you get the crew to clear up the trash and make this place look decent, please? I'll make sure you guys get time and a half until the new guy gets here."

"That's cool, Boss. I'll get the guys on it right away." He called in rapid Spanish to his crew as he walked away.

Hugh let him go, then turned back to the trailer in time to see Mark's car fishtail out of the lot, spewing a cloud of dust and gravel in its wake. Good riddance. He had to find a new superintendent for this site, preferably before lunch. He logged on to the computer in the trailer and was searching through employment records when his cell buzzed. "Yeah. This is Hugh."

"Hey. It's Dino at the Petroglyphs site." Dino was the superintendent at their newest site on the far West Mesa where they were just now breaking ground for a housing development. It was about as far west of Albuquerque as you could get without actually living in Grants, eighty miles from the city.

Hugh had a sinking feeling; there was no reason for the superintendent to call him if everything was going well. "Yeah, Dino. What's up?"

"We got a problem, Hugh. Backhoe dug up some bones this morning. Human, by the looks of them."

"Aww, shit."

"Yeah, for sure."

"I can be there in about twenty minutes." God, when it rained, it poured. He called to Bob and loaded him into the truck. The day had started out on such a promising note. Twenty-five minutes later he pulled into the empty lot that would someday soon become the newest DeLuca Homes development. The crew was standing around the backhoe, smoking, talking, and pointing at an area of disturbed dirt. "Okay, Dino. What have we got?"

Dino waved him over and pointed.

Hugh looked and saw cream-colored bones exposed in the dirt pile directly in front of the backhoe.

"Maybe we uncovered an ancient Indian burial site," Dino said. "They might get archeologists from the university out here. That could mess up this job site for a long time, man."

Hugh said nothing, but crouched down next to the bones and brushed the dirt away from the skull. "I doubt it's all that ancient." The skull was largely intact and clearly showed a small round hole in the center of the forehead. "Goddammit," he muttered as he pulled his phone from his pocket. She answered on the third ring. "Chrissy? Yeah, it's Hugh. I need your help."

***

Chris

While it wasn't exactly the type of phone call she was hoping for from Hugh, it was something. It took her nearly forty-five minutes to get from her precinct to the vacant lot where his crew had unearthed human bones. She had no idea what to expect, but Hugh had seemed confident it was a human skull he'd seen. He turned and walked to her car as she pulled into the lot; her stomach clenched at the sight of him, as it had every single time she'd so much as caught a glimpse of the man. She hadn't experienced a crush this bad since high school and wasn't sure she liked it. It made her feel weak and girly. But God, he was so handsome and such a nice guy!

"Hey, Chrissy." He held his hand out to help her

out of the car.

When was the last time someone had done that for her? Ever? "Hi." She put her hand in his, loving the warm, rough feel of his skin. "Let's see your body."

He raised his eyebrows, one corner of his mouth raised in amusement.

"The one in the ground. The bones." God, what was wrong with her?

"That's a relief. I'd hate to strip down in front of the crew."

"Shut up."

He laughed and led her toward the backhoe. "Dino, this is Lieutenant Hart with the State Police. Chrissy, this is Dino Avila. He's the superintendent on this job."

"Hello, ma'am." They shook hands and Dino led her to where the bones were sticking out of the ground. "We found them this morning. I thought maybe we found an old Indian burial ground or something, but Hugh doesn't think so."

She smiled briefly at the man and squatted down next to bones. She could make out a skull, and Hugh had been right: there was a small round hole clearly visible in the dead center of the forehead. She stood and dusted her hands on her jeans. "Okay. I'm going to call in a forensic unit and see what we're dealing with here."

Forty-five minutes later, the forensic unit arrived and began setting up. She watched as they began the process of fully unearthing the bones. She stood to the side as they worked, carefully sifting through the dirt. She had removed her blazer and now rolled up the sleeves of her white shirt. Albuquerque was experiencing an Indian summer and it was hot, even though it was already October.

"Here." Hugh handed her a bottle of cold water. "You want to come sit in the office for a bit? We've got the air conditioning on in there. Looks like this is going to take a while."

She uncapped the bottle and drank deeply. "Thanks. Yeah, I'd love to get out of this sun for a while." She followed him up the steps into the construction office. Inside it was strictly utilitarian, with metal desks, folding chairs, and file cabinets. Hugh pulled a chair out for her and wiped the seat with a paper towel before she sat, a courtesy she hadn't expected. "Thanks."

He smiled down at her as she sat. "So, this takes a lot longer than it does on television."

She chuckled. "Oh, yeah. Real police investigations aren't terribly glamorous. I'm sorry for what this must be doing to your construction schedule."

"Well, I won't pretend I'm thrilled, but I sent the crew over to another job that needs some extra help, so it's okay. Any idea how long I'll need to keep this one shut down?"

"No, sorry. It depends a lot on what they find."

"So, is this pretty typical? What else does a detective do all day? I'm really curious." He pulled a folding chair next to her and sat, straddling it, resting his arms along the back.

She was instantly distracted by the sight of those tan arms, sculpted and corded with veins, visible below his rolled-up sleeves. A tantalizing vee of his chest peeked out as well, with a hint of dark chest hair. She sipped her water more to hide any possible drooling than because she was thirsty. "Your brother is a detective. Haven't you grilled him about what we do all day?"

He flashed her a grin. "I'm not interested in what my brother does all day. I'd much rather hear it from his gorgeous partner."

He was flirting with her. She didn't know what to say or do; it had been way too long since anyone had flirted with her. She wished she was one of those women who could respond in like manner and flirt back, letting him know she was interested. Instead, she felt the heat rising up her neck and feared her face was turning a lovely beet red. She fumbled her water bottle, managing to spill some on her shirt.

He stood and crossed the room to get her a paper towel. "Here. Do I make you nervous, Chrissy?"

"No, of course not. Why should you make me nervous?" She ineffectively mopped at her shirt with one hand.

"I shouldn't. Friends shouldn't make each other nervous."

Her heart thudded dully. *Friends. Of course.* He'd even placed a slight emphasis on the word, hadn't he? Well, message received. "No, of course not." After all, having him as a friend was better than nothing.

"Good. Now, what do you do all day? I've seen you interrogate a suspect, and I've seen you blaze into a horrible situation, but I suspect your job involves a lot more."

"Yes, thankfully. I don't typically go around shooting people on a daily basis." He'd been with her when she arrived on the scene a few months ago to find Mel and Finn's neighbor, Lena, holding a gun on both of them, about to shoot. The woman had fixated on Finn after a brief encounter they'd had at a bar; Finn had been drunk and didn't even remember her, while Lena built an obsession about him that ended in Chris shooting her before she could kill Finn. Lena lived through it and was now awaiting trial. Thankfully, the judge had recognized the danger she represented and refused to set bail. She was safely incarcerated in the Bernalillo County Metro Detention Center.

"Hey." He reached out and took her hand, holding it loosely while he rubbed his thumb across her fingers. "You saved my brother's life, and possibly my sister-in-law's life. I'll never forget that, Chrissy."

She gulped and stared at their clasped hands. It was so hard to be okay with 'just friends' when he was touching her. "Yeah, well, decent partners are hard to come by. I didn't want to lose the one I've got. Actually, I spend a whole lot of my time writing reports. Most people don't realize how much writing cops have to do."

"It's the same with construction, at least when you're the boss. I swear I write more than I ever did in college! I would have paid more attention in my English classes if I'd known."

"I wrote a twenty-seven-page report last week."

"Ouch." He winced and squeezed her hand lightly. "That's brutal. Maybe we—"

But one of the forensic techs came in at that moment, smirking as he noticed their clasped hands. Chris hastily dropped Hugh's hand and stood. "What have you found, Mike?"

"Two more bodies. Looks like there could be more." He led them outside where the crime scene had been enlarged and more techs were crouched and sprawled, brushing dirt away from more exposed bones.

She left Hugh under the shade canopy the techs had set up and strode to the newest area uncovered. Who knew how many bodies were here? It was patently obvious they weren't dealing with any ancient Indian burial ground, but she had no idea what it was. Each of the three skulls had identical holes in the center of the forehead, which screamed execution-style killing. God, what a mess! And now the techs were telling her they couldn't get what they needed to do their job. She pulled her phone out of her back pocket and punched buttons violently. She finally got through to someone in charge of requisitions. "Yeah, well, I don't give a shit about backlogs! Get me a fucking ground-penetrating radar unit now! You tell him it's on the authority of Lieutenant Hart." She clicked off and stormed away to talk to the man in charge of the forensic team.

It was nearing three o'clock by the time she had five minutes to call her own. She exited the tiny bathroom in the construction trailer office to find Hugh setting sub sandwiches and chips out on his desk.

"Come have some lunch, Chrissy. You must be

41

starving."

"Thanks, but I'll eat later. My guys will be hungry too."

"I ordered lunch for everyone. They're eating already. Come sit down for a few minutes." He held his hand out for her.

She surrendered, glad to get off her feet for a while. "Thanks, Hugh. This is really nice. Most crime scenes don't come with lunch."

He chuckled and handed her a soda. "Well, we'll have to try it again sometime without the crime scene."

She froze, a chip halfway to her mouth. *Did he just ask me out?* "Sure. Sounds great." She ate the chip and reached for the soda. She spent the rest of the time concentrating on eating without knocking anything over or spilling her drink. She mostly succeeded, but hurried through her food so she could get back to work.

By five o'clock they'd brought in the ground penetrating radar, which showed at least two more bodies nearby. Hugh had retreated to the trailer, so she went to find him. He looked up when she walked in. She straddled the chair she'd sat in earlier. "Hey. Why don't you go home? We'll be a few more hours."

He walked around his desk and came to stand behind her. He put his hands on her shoulders, rubbing and massaging the tension in her neck. "Okay, but why don't you come by when you get done? I'll grill you a steak and you can fill me in on the rest of this shit storm."

She laughed and let her head loll. God, his hands

were magical. "It could be late. I'll need to stop by Finn's place and feed the animals."

"Doesn't matter. After the day you've had, you need a good meal and some decent wine. And I'll go by and feed Fluff and CJ. I'll even take Fluff to my place so he's not alone so long."

"You don't know how good that sounds."

"Great, then I'll see you in a few hours. I'll text you my address."

She followed him out of the trailer and watched him drive away in his truck, Bob in the back of the king cab. She watched the dust chase his vehicle down the road then turned to the officers working the crime scene. "All right, guys! Let's get this wrapped up, pronto!" She had a date and she wasn't about to miss it.

Chapter Four

Hugh

"Hugh? Is that you?"

"Yeah, Mom." He closed the kitchen door of his parents' house behind him and found his mother at the sink, washing dishes. Delicious smells filled the room and Hugh guessed it was pot roast night. Bob trotted off to locate Hugh's father, who always managed to find a treat for him. Bob knew this and was gifted at manipulating him. "Don't you have a dishwasher?" He put an arm around her shoulders and kissed the top of her head.

"It's such a waste to run it for just a few dishes. Have you eaten yet, dear? Let me set a place for you." Her voice still held a lovely Irish lilt regardless of the fact she'd lived in the United States for more than thirty years.

"No thanks. I'm going to stop by the grocery store on my way home and pick something up."

"Oh, sweetie, that's not necessary. I hate that you eat alone every night." She turned and opened a cabinet. "I fixed plenty."

Hugh rolled his eyes—behind her back, of course—and gently closed the cabinet. "I won't be alone tonight."

She stared up at him, a slow smile spreading across her face as comprehension dawned. "You have a date?"

It was his mother's dearest desire in life to see each of her six children happily married and busily producing grandchildren for her to spoil. Finn was currently at the top of her favorite child list for getting married last week. "Sort of, but it's extremely early days yet, so don't get excited."

"What's her name?"

"Nope. My lips are sealed until I see how it goes, okay?" He certainly didn't want to tell his mother his date was with Chrissy. She had grown fond of Finn's partner during the wedding planning, not to mention the fact that Chrissy had saved Finn's life. His mother would be over the moon if she knew Hugh had the hots for her, but he wasn't ready to go public with it quite yet. "I need to talk to Dad about something."

"He's in the den, probably feeding your dog potato chips or something."

He was feeding Bob bits of Moira's homemade peanut butter cookies. Hugh grabbed one off the plate and flopped onto the sofa. "You're going to get him fat, Dad."

"So take him for a run. He likes cookies, don't you, Bob? Yeah, you love to come visit Grandpa, don't you?"

God, his parents needed more grandkids. He'd be

happy to get busy with that, but a wife would make it a heck of lot easier. He didn't envy Izzy in her role as a single parent. And he didn't want any old wife, either. He wanted someone special, someone who would be a best friend, a companion, a lover for the rest of their lives. Was it supposed to be this hard? "I stopped by to let you know we're putting a bid in on the Kensington job tomorrow."

"Good. What number did you come up with?"

They talked shop for a while; Hugh knew his father enjoyed being kept in the loop even though he'd retired nearly four years ago and handed the company over to his eldest son and daughter. They all had hopes the youngest DeLuca, Tony, would eventually join them when he finished his business degree. Finn, Cara, and Seamus had all found other occupations and passions to follow, but Hugh had always felt drawn to the family business and had never regretted his decision to work for his father during and after college. Now with his father's retirement, he and Izzy were determined to take the construction company to the next level.

He left his parents' house and stopped by the grocery store to pick up porterhouse steaks, potatoes, and a nice merlot. He added some salad fixings as an afterthought. Chrissy would probably appreciate something healthy. Once home, he put the steaks in the fridge to marinate, wrapped the potatoes in foil and stuck them in the oven, and set to work on the salad. He knew he was fussing, trying to impress the woman, and he wasn't even sure he wanted to pursue a relationship with her. He set the knife down next to the tomato he was chopping and closed his eyes, gripping the edge of the countertop hard. He needed to stop lying to himself. He definitely wanted to pursue a relationship with her, but he didn't know if it was a good idea. He wasn't sure she wanted the same things from life he did...and he was desperately afraid to ask her. *Okay, idiot. She's coming over here tonight and you need to make a decision. Are you going to let her know you how you feel, or are you going to chicken out? She deserves to know, one way or another. If you're not going to make a move, then you need to let her go. Stop dicking around with her.*

The doorbell rang, startling him. She was earlier than he'd expected and he wasn't ready. He'd planned to shower and change, but it was too late. *Shit.* He wiped his suddenly sweaty hands on his jeans and forced himself to walk to the door. "Hey, I didn't expect you for at least—" His brother, Tony, was on the other side of the door.

"Hey, Hugh." He pushed his way past his brother and made himself at home on the sofa, pausing to pet Fluff, who was curled up on the couch, and Bob, who was on the floor next to him. "I was in the area and figured I'd stop by so we could watch the game together on your big-ass TV. I brought beer." He reached for the remote. "Why don't you have it on yet? We've missed the first down. And why is Mel's dog here?"

Hugh had completely forgotten about the Broncos game and chose to ignore the question about Fluff. It wasn't unusual for him and his brothers to get together, frequently at his house since he had a 60-inch flat screen with surround sound. But tonight was not going to work for him. He needed to get rid of his brother fast. He ran through various scenarios in his head and rejected most of them, finally settling for the truth. Or a reasonable facsimile of it. He reached for the remote and clicked the television off.

"Hey! What the hell?"

"I need you to leave, Tony. I'm expecting someone any minute."

The grin spreading across Tony's face was absolutely evil. "Ohhh. Do tell, brother." He reclined and twisted the top off a beer.

"Not gonna happen, Tony. Get your ass out of here before my date arrives."

"But I'm so comfortable here, Hugh. I don't have homework tonight and I want to spend some quality time with my big brother. I've missed you." His eyes were large blue orbs over the top of his beer.

Hugh crossed his arms and frowned at the younger man. "Hmm. I'm trying to decide which episode Mom would rather hear about first: the one where you called me from jail or the one where I found you naked in bed with two equally naked girls when you had the house to yourself for the weekend last year."

Tony choked on a sip of beer and stood. "I had permission to be in that house! And I only remember going to bed with one of those girls, I swear!"

Hugh didn't say anything.

"Okay, fine! I'm going! Jeez, you don't have to

get so cranky! I can't believe you, of all people, would stoop to blackmail. You think you know a guy." He stuffed the remaining five beers in the brown paper bag. "But I'm taking my beer with me."

Hugh saw him to the door.

Tony turned at the last minute. "It's not Lauren, is it? You guys getting back together?"

Not in a million years. "Goodnight, Tony."

"Yeah, I'm going." He turned and headed down the walkway.

It would have been perfect if Chrissy hadn't pulled into his driveway at that moment. Hugh sighed as Tony swiveled his head back and forth between the two of them, a slow grin spreading across his face.

"Well, hey there, Chris. Fancy meeting you here." Tony's tone was gleeful.

"Hi, Tony. It's nice to see you again." She glanced between the brothers, uncertainty written across her features.

"Tony was just leaving. Remember what we talked about, Tony."

"Yeah, yeah. Have fun, you two! Don't do anything I wouldn't!"

Hugh figured that left a whole lot of territory open to him. "Hi, Chrissy." She looked exhausted, but still gorgeous. "Come on in." He led her through to the kitchen and motioned for her to sit at the bar while he poured her a glass of the merlot.

"Sláinte." She raised her glass. "Did I say it right?"

He grinned, enchanted anew. "Close enough.

You must be starving."

"I could eat."

***

Chris

She'd been disappointed when she arrived and found Tony already there. She'd hoped Hugh had meant his invitation as something of a date. But if he had also invited siblings, it was more of a get-together. But then he'd basically kicked his younger brother out, and she'd felt a surge of renewed optimism. *Stupid. Don't get your hopes up, girl.* But she couldn't help it. She watched him chopping a tomato and enjoyed the way his muscular shoulders moved as he worked the knife. She imagined him doing it shirtless and smiled.

He chose that moment to turn and look at her, of course. He raised his eyebrows, as if asking what she was grinning like a fool about.

"You have a nice house," she blurted.

He grinned return. "You want the nickel tour?"

"Sure."

He held out his hand and helped her up. "This, of course, is the kitchen. It doesn't get a lot of action, but the fridge and microwave do amazing things with leftover pizza."

She laughed and glanced around at the spacious room, envying the top of the line appliances and counter space. Her kitchen was a small hallway. It made cooking a chore. "You don't like to cook?"

"I don't hate it, but I'm not very good. Finn got

all the kitchen talent from our mother." He had retained her hand and now pulled her through to the living room. Bob and Fluff followed, tails wagging.

"That's a big TV."

"Yeah. It's very popular with my brothers."

The room was large and comfortable. The dark brown overstuffed sofa looked like a great place for an afternoon nap. The coffee table held an assortment of sports magazines. Framed pictures of his family graced many of the surfaces, with an entire section devoted to his young niece, Janey. The room wasn't messy, but neither was it fussily neat. He'd used various shades of blue as an accent and she wondered if it was his favorite color. A large dog bed and a basket of chew toys was tucked away in a corner.

"Upstairs we have the master bedroom and bath." He led her up the curving flight of stairs and into his bedroom. The king-size bed was made, although a bit lumpy, and the room smelled like him, a mixture of his aftershave, soap, and masculinity. Another dog bed and a smaller toy basket filled the space next to the bed.

She inhaled deeply, trying not to be too obvious about it. She wished she could bottle that scent. There was a large, jetted tub in the bathroom, and she imagined herself submerged, bubbles up to her chin, with a glass of wine and candles around the perimeter. There were two smaller bedrooms across the hall. He used one as a home office and the other was a guest room. A toy box in the corner and a large dollhouse told her Janey was his most frequent visitor. "This is certainly not your stereotypical bachelor pad."

He smiled and tugged her out of the room. "I like to think I'm not your stereotypical bachelor. Let me show you the backyard."

It was gorgeous, with a green lawn, a small pool, and a Jacuzzi. "God, that hot tub looks amazing right now." The afternoon had been endless as she stood in the baking sun, waiting for the forensic team to finish. She always put all her stress in her shoulders and today had been incredibly stressful. She would love to be able to let all the tightness and stress float away in his hot tub.

"Feel free. You could have a nice long soak while I grill the steaks."

"Sounds great, but I don't have my suit," she said with a sigh.

"Suits are totally optional here. I can't promise I won't peek, though." He grinned and winked at her.

She laughed at his outrageous flirting. "Maybe next time. For now, how about if I just drink some more wine and watch you grill?"

"Spoilsport. Have a seat. I'll be right back."

They ate on the patio in the cool of the evening. The steaks were delicious and he'd cooked hers exactly the way she liked with a deep pink center. She started to tell him where they were with the investigation, but he suggested they talk about more pleasant things during dinner.

"I asked you here so you could relax, Chrissy. You can tell me about that other stuff tomorrow. You're off the clock for tonight." He poured her another glass of wine. "Tell me about growing up in El Paso."

"It was hot."

He raised his eyebrows and frowned. "That's it? I want details."

She chuckled self-consciously; it was difficult to let her guard down and talk about herself. "Well, my younger sister and I were very close. She's only eighteen months younger, so we always played together. We grew more apart in high school when we developed different interests, then I came here for college and never left."

"Did you always want to be a cop?"

She smiled and shook her head. "Don't laugh, but I always planned to be a doctor."

"And you changed your mind because...?"

"Because the science classes they make you take were too hard. I hated them! All I ever did was study. I really liked my criminology elective, though. So, I took another one. And then another. Pretty soon I was a criminology major. After I graduated, it seemed logical to apply for the police academy."

"Finn said you hold the record for making detective at the youngest age."

"Yeah, but he almost beat me. He's a great partner. I've only had one other, but Finn is better."

"He says you're a great partner too."

"We work well together. He charms the ladies and I can pull off the sympathy for the guys. Makes them spill their guts every time."

"I've seen you do that. Yeah, Finn oozes charm. It pisses me off sometimes. It's always tended to get him what he wants."

She laughed at his grumpiness. "Oh, you're

plenty charming yourself, mister. It's subtler than Finn's, but it's definitely there."

"Good to know." He flashed her one his charming smiles, making her stomach flip.

"So, what about you? Tell me about your childhood. What was it like being the oldest of six? I can't begin to imagine the chaos."

"Oh, it wasn't too bad. I did a lot of babysitting, though. I was twelve when Tony was born and horribly embarrassed that my mother and father were apparently still having sex."

She laughed, nearly snorting her wine. "You and Izzy are the oldest, right?"

He nodded. "She's your age. Finn and I were the closest growing up, though. Poor Izzy; she was pretty lonely until Cara got big enough to play with."

"Was she married? I've never heard anything about Janey's father."

He shook his head. "Nope. Cara's the only one who has been married. Well, until Finn, of course. Izzy won't tell anyone who Janey's father is. It's a big mystery."

"I had no idea Cara was married. They're divorced?"

"Yeah. His name was Aidan and they were high school sweethearts. He basically went nuts after they got married. She never said much about it but we could all tell she wasn't happy. You've never been married, have you?"

She shook her head. "I lived with a guy, Greg, for two years. I always thought we'd eventually get married, but…"

"But?"

She smiled crookedly and sipped her wine. "He didn't want to. I finally gave him an ultimatum: either we get married or the relationship was over. I was tired of spinning my wheels." She set her glass down and grimaced. "He moved out the next day."

"I'm sorry. His loss."

"What about you? Finn said you had a long-term girlfriend, but it didn't work out."

"Lauren. We were together five years. We were engaged, briefly, at the very end. Finn doesn't know that."

"I won't say anything." She could tell from his closed expression he didn't want to talk about it any longer. It was obviously still a sore subject and she wondered if he was still carrying a torch for his ex. "Dinner was delicious. Thanks, Hugh."

"I've got another bottle of wine. It's still pretty early."

"No. I have to drive home and they frown on cops getting pulled over for DWI. This has been wonderful, though. I needed it after the day I had. It's been a long time since anyone asked me out." She winced as she realized how that sounded. She thought of this as a date, but she didn't want him to think she assumed it was. "I mean, I know this wasn't a date or anything, but—"

Hugh reached to cover her hand with his own. "Chrissy. I had every intention of this being a date. Unless you don't want it to be a date?"

Her heart pounded so hard she was sure he would hear it. "I'm okay with a date."

He smiled and stood, pulling her with him. "If I

wasn't clear about that, I apologize. This is a date, and I fervently hope there will be others." He pushed her long bangs behind her ear, letting his hand cup her cheek. "And unless you stop me, I'm going to kiss you."

She swallowed hard and licked her suddenly dry lips. "Okay."

"Okay yes? Or okay no?"

She didn't answer. Instead she stepped closer and angled her head, reaching up slightly to lay her lips on his. The kiss was soft and his lips remained still for a moment. She pulled back slightly and smiled. "Okay yes."

He grinned and pulled her against him. Then his lips were back on hers, and this time they weren't still. His mouth was warm and his tongue soon sought entrance between her lips.

She gladly obliged, enthralled by the silky feel of his mouth and the heady taste of him, a blend of wine and the dark chocolate he'd served for dessert. She wrapped her arms around him and held tightly while he swept her into a maelstrom of feeling. God, this man could kiss! She felt it all the way down to her toes and all the good parts in between. She answered as best she could, letting her tongue tangle with his and nibbling his full lower lip.

He pulled away far too soon and rested his forehead against hers. "You are a fantastic kisser, Chrissy. Wow."

She grinned at him. "I was thinking the exact same thing about you."

"Well, it seems like we should probably explore our talents a bit more." He kissed her again, softly.

"Go out with me. Tomorrow?"
She nodded. "It's a date."

Chapter Five

Hugh

He was absorbed in finishing the bid for the Kensington job when his intercom buzzed. He pressed the button absently with barely a glance. "Yeah, Malva?"

"Hugh, there's a Detective Hart here to see you."

The Kensington job was instantly forgotten. "Send her in, please." He knew it would be cooler to wait for her at his desk, looking busy and professional, but he was too excited to see her. He reached the door just as Malva opened it and motioned Chrissy inside.

"Good morning, Mr. DeLuca. I was hoping you might have a few minutes to see me. I have some information on the bodies you found yesterday." Chrissy held out her hand to shake his.

He raised his eyebrows, amused at her formal tone. Apparently, she was trying to keep their relationship a secret. Well, he'd play along, although he was ready to go public now that he'd finally decided to pursue the relationship and she seemed amenable. He had nothing to hide anymore and would gladly inform Finn as soon as he got back from his honeymoon. "I think I could squeeze you in...Detective Hark, was it?"

"Hart." She flashed an annoyed look at him.

He ushered her into his office, grinning behind her back. He closed the door and contemplated pulling her into his arms and kissing her senseless. Or at least until she remembered his first name. It was probably way too early in their relationship to do that, though. *Screw it. I need to kiss her.* He grabbed her hand and spun her back around and into his arms.

"Wha—?"

He forestalled anything else she might have said by crushing his mouth against hers. He'd wondered if perhaps the kiss the night before had been a fluke. Surely it hadn't been as amazing as he remembered. She caught up with him and softened her mouth under his, opening to his questing tongue. Nope. It definitely hadn't been a fluke.

"Hugh," she breathed.

He grinned against her lips. "Ah, so you do remember my first name. Good." He kissed her again, sinking into the bliss of her incredible mouth. He finally groaned and pulled away reluctantly. Much more of this and he'd do something really stupid, like pushing her down on the sofa and taking her in the middle of his office. With his luck, Izzy would choose that exact moment to burst in unannounced. Since it wasn't the way he would choose to announce their relationship, he guided her to sit and took a chair next to her. "So," he said as he cleared his throat, "you have some info on the bodies?"

"Um, bodies?" She had a gratifyingly dazed look on her face. Bob dragged himself away from his new chew toy and approached her, his entire body quivering with excitement. She took his head between her palms and leaned down to kiss him on the nose, laughing when his long tongue snaked out and slurped her chin.

Hugh felt a pang in his chest, somewhere in the region of his heart. *I could fall in love with her.* He waited for the panic to follow this realization, but it never came. All he felt was contentment. He stood and crossed to the coffeemaker, pouring them each a cup before he returned to her side. "Here. Sorry about attacking you the second you walked in. I missed you."

She glanced up from the dog with a wry smile. "I don't mind." She sipped her coffee. "I missed you too. I could have called, but I wanted to see you."

Izzy chose that moment to enter, without knocking, of course. "Chris! Malva said Hugh was with a Detective Hart, so I figured I'd join you so I can hear what's new with the investigation. Hugh told me all about it yesterday." She glanced between the two and seemed to pick up on the underlying current. "I feel like I've interrupted something."

Chrissy laughed awkwardly. "No, of course not."

Hugh rolled his eyes slightly, but held his tongue for the moment. He wouldn't say anything until he knew Chrissy was okay with his family knowing they were dating. "So, what have you discovered?"

She flashed him a grateful glance and sat up, once again the professional detective. "There are a total of six bodies, all male, all shot point blank in the forehead. Preliminary autopsy results place them in the age range of 25-40. The bodies have been in the ground for at least thirty years."

"How horrible! Who are—I mean were—they?" Izzy asked.

"We haven't been able to make an ID on any of the bodies yet. That's going to be tough, given how long ago they were killed."

"Why is that?" Izzy continued her interrogation.

Chrissy smiled at her and answered patiently. "CODIS, the DNA database, wasn't begun until the late 90s. We'll still run their DNA, but it will be a miracle if we find anything. Unfortunately, we found no papers or any kind of identification on them."

"So, there's no way to figure out who they were?" Izzy looked upset at the thought.

"We have a few other tricks up our sleeves, but it will probably take quite a while."

"How long until we can get back to building houses on the site?" Hugh was sympathetic to the police investigation, but he had a business to run.

Chrissy smiled sympathetically. "It will be a few weeks. I'm sorry, Hugh."

He saw Izzy glance up quickly, frowning. She flashed him a questioning glance, which he pretended not to notice. "It's not your fault. I'll assign the crew to other sites for the time being."

Izzy was still frowning, as if she couldn't quite

understand what was going on. "Hey, Chris, you want to get together tonight? I can see if Cara's free and if Mom can watch Janey. We could go shopping and grab dinner somewhere. We haven't had a chance to do that since before the wedding."

The shocked look on Chrissy's face was amusing. "Oh. I can't tonight. Sorry. I have a uh, a date."

"Really? How exciting! What's his name?"

Chrissy glanced quickly at Hugh, a plea for help clearly written across her features.

He sighed inwardly. Well, what the hell? Tony already knew, and he'd never be able to keep his mouth shut, so it might as well come out now. "Hugh. His name is Hugh." He reached for Chrissy's hand as he spoke.

The shock on Izzy's face was priceless. "Oh. My. God!" She finished on a small squeal, rather unusual for her. "How long has this been going on?"

"Calm down, Iz, okay? It's pretty recent, and we haven't exactly gone public yet. We would like to tell people ourselves, especially Finn, so if you could—" Hugh could see his sister bubbling with excitement.

"Of course. I won't say a thing! Does Cara know?"

"Only Tony knows, because the idiot showed up at my house unexpectedly last night." He stood, ready to end the mini-inquisition, as much for Chrissy's sake as his own. "Now, if you don't mind, I'd like to say goodbye to Chrissy. Alone."

Izzy grinned and stood, launching herself at him

for a hug. "I'm so happy for you, Hugh." She whispered the words.

"I know." She'd been there to help pick up the pieces when his last relationship fell apart, understanding he was devastated, even though she didn't know all the details. No one did, except him and Lauren. He'd chosen not to tell his family what had really happened; it was simply too painful. He felt his gut cramp as he remembered and banished the thoughts. They had no place in his very new relationship with Chrissy.

Izzy excused herself hastily, shutting the office door behind her.

"Sorry about that. I didn't know what to say." Chrissy looked adorably unsure of herself.

"There's nothing to be sorry about. It would have been fun to keep you all to myself for a bit longer, but Tony already knew, which means Seamus probably knows. I doubt Izzy will be able to keep it from Cara." He chuckled as he pulled her into his arms. "My family is a nightmare. You might want to run while you still can."

"Are you trying to get rid of me?"

He leaned in to kiss her softly, enjoying that he didn't have to bend his head far to do it. She fit against him so well and he loved the feel of her strong body pressing against his. "Not even close." He felt something vibrating from the region of her rear end.

She reached into her back pocket and retrieved her cell phone. "Sorry." She mouthed the words as she answered. "This is Hart."

He loosened his hold on her as she listened, but

didn't release her completely. He liked the feel of her in his arms and wondered why he hadn't had the good sense to make his move months ago.

"Will do. Thanks for the update." She clicked off and stuffed the phone back in her pocket. "I gotta go. The autopsies are under way and we've got some bullet fragments."

"And that's a good thing?"

She smiled. "It may help us ID the bodies. Maybe." She kissed him quickly and turned to go. "See you tonight?"

"I'll pick you up at seven."

***

Chris

She worked through lunch so she would be able to take off early enough to get home and shower and shave her legs before tonight's date. Not that she was expecting to have any reason for shaved legs, but still. She hadn't been on a date in more than six months and she was planning to enjoy this one. It helped that she was already half in love with the guy. God, when he'd pulled her into his arms earlier in his office you could have knocked her over with a feather! She'd never expected him to be so spontaneous. He'd always been so reserved and guarded around her, but she apparently had a lot to learn about him. She could hardly wait.

"What are you grinning about, Hart?" Darren Gonzales, one of the other detectives, swiveled his chair around and stared.

"None of your goddamn business, Gonzales. Don't you have anything better to do than annoy me?" She would have to be more careful to keep her emotions hidden. It was hard enough being a woman in this field without running the risk of exposing her love life to her colleagues. They would be ruthless with their teasing.

"Jeez. How come you're so cranky? You missing your partner?"

"I'm not cranky. And yes, I miss Finn. I'm sick to death of doing all the paperwork around here while he's basking in the sun all day."

"If he's sunbathing all day on his honeymoon, he's dumber than I thought." He snickered and turned back to his desk.

Chris rolled her eyes and returned to her report. Her stomach growled and she took a moment to fish through her desk drawers to see if she had anything to nibble. She found a slightly stale packet of cheese crackers and munched absently while she finished the preliminary report on the bodies found on Hugh's job site. Her captain expected an update by three and she was running behind. She shouldn't have taken the time to visit Hugh that morning, but the thought of seeing him had been irresistible. *Focus, girl!* She had stopped by afterward to talk with the medical examiner and pick up the bullet fragments he'd found in the bodies so she could send them to the lab for ballistic fingerprinting. With any luck, they'd get something to go on from them. She was keeping her fingers crossed, but the length of time the bodies had been in the ground made it doubtful they'd find anything.

65

She finally wrapped everything up around five-thirty and rushed to Finn's house to get ready for her date. She'd stopped by her apartment earlier to pick up clothes, since she hadn't taken anything dressy to Finn and Mel's. She'd grabbed several possibilities and stowed them in the backseat of her car. She flew through the shower, making sure to use her cherry blossom shower gel and matching lotion afterward. She might work in a male-dominated field, but she enjoyed feminine clothes and scents in her off hours. She'd cut her hair short a few years ago, thinking people might take her more seriously, but found she liked it for the most part. She wondered if Hugh liked it, and then chastised herself for caring what any guy thought. But she wondered, all the same. She stood in front of the closet in the guest room, clad only in the matching lace bra and panty set she'd been saving for a special occasion—not that she expected Hugh to see it tonight—and agonized over what to wear. She had no idea where he would take her, and thus no clue how she should dress. Albuquerque was casual in the extreme, so she'd probably be okay pretty much anywhere with a nice dress. Plus, she wanted to make sure her legs were showing. She'd been told they were one of her best features, so she wanted to choose something that would show them off. After pulling three different dresses out and discarding them, she finally settled on her go-to little black dress she knew looked good. She added her favorite pair of strappy heels, glad Hugh was so tall. She loved wearing high heels, but usually felt conspicuous and enormous. She wore the diamond studs her parents had given her when she made detective, but no other jewelry. She checked the clock on her nightstand and realized she had ten minutes to spare. She'd hoped to take every spare second, but nerves must have made her rush. *Crap. I didn't want extra time to sit and get nervous.* She left her bedroom and went to wait impatiently on Mel's sofa. Fluff hopped up beside her, but CJ stayed where she was, curled up on a recliner. What if he arrives wearing jeans and a t-shirt? Do I look like I'm trying too hard? Maybe I should change into something more casual. The knock on the door saved her from freaking out about it further.

"Hey, I'm sorry I'm—" Whatever else he'd been about to say froze as he stood with his mouth hanging open.

"Hi. What's wrong?" She was concerned, as he remained stock-still.

He shook his head. "Nothing. Nothing at all. Wow." He gave her a once-over and smiled. "You look amazing, Chrissy. Wow."

"Thanks. You look great too." He was wearing dark dress slacks and a teal shirt, open at the throat. "Come in." She stepped aside to let him in. She shut the door and they stood awkwardly for several moments. "I didn't know where we were going, so I hope this is okay." She gestured to her dress.

He smiled and stepped close to her. "You look perfect." He leaned in and kissed her cheek. "I made reservations at Antiquity. I hope that's all right."

She was glad she'd decided to go with the black dress. She'd never been to Antiquity, an upscale restaurant in Albuquerque's Old Town. It was way above her pay grade. "Um, yeah. It sounds great. I've never been."

"Let's go then. If you're ready?"

She nodded and picked up her purse. They walked to the driveway together and she was surprised to see a silver BMW. "Where's your truck?"

He held the passenger door for her and jogged around to get in the driver's side. "My truck is for work. I also left Bob home tonight." He smiled and winked at her.

Good lord! Business must be good for DeLuca Construction. She admitted to herself she was a bit intimidated. It didn't get any better when he pulled to the front of the beautiful adobe restaurant and allowed the valet to park his car. Once inside, they were seated in a quiet corner booth. She was used to looking for the cheapest thing on the menu, but sensed she needn't do that with Hugh. Neither did she want to order the most expensive dinner, either. He suggested the Chateaubriand for two and ordered a bottle of Cabernet. They shared a Creme Brûlée for dessert, along with coffee. She was careful not to overeat, not wanting to look like a pig or start oozing out of her dress, but it was hard because it was delicious. She'd been worried they might not have anything to talk about during dinner, but her worries were groundless; they talked non-stop, laughing frequently. He was smart and funny, and she found herself relaxed and able to enjoy herself.

"Tell me something you don't like, Chrissy." He

poured them each a final glass of wine as he spoke.

"Why?"

"Suspicious much? Because what you don't like says a lot about a person."

"Olives."

He chuckled and set down his wine. "Olives, huh? You seem fairly passionate about your dislike."

"It's more of a hatred. They're disgusting. So, what does that tell you about me?"

"Hmm. Well, it tells me intriguing things about the depths of your passions, which I look forward to learning about in the future. Personally, I'm conflicted. The Italian half of me is appalled. Mediterranean cooking features a lot of olives. The Irish half of me is fine with it, however. The Irish have little use for olives."

She laughed. "You like olives, huh?"

"Love them. But I've been told I'm a bit of an olive snob. I don't go for the rubbery, canned sort."

"If I had to guess, I'd go with one of your brothers informing you of your snobbery."

"Bingo. Seamus frequently lets me know I'm a snob of one sort or another. He seems to take great pleasure in doing it."

"So tell me something you don't like." She was curious now that he'd brought it up. She wondered if he'd say something innocuous, as she had, or something deeper.

He reached for her hand on the table top and met her gaze. "I don't like thinking about the kind of danger you face in your job."

She clasped his warm hand and squeezed.

69

"That's sweet, Hugh. My job's not terribly dangerous now that I'm a detective. It's mostly paperwork and puzzles. I hardly ever even pull my gun these days."

"Did you mean to kill her?" He referred to the occasion a few months previously when she'd pulled her gun and shot Lena before the woman could shoot Finn or Mel.

She smiled wryly and pulled her hand away. "We're trained to shoot to stop the perp. That frequently means death, but not always or necessarily. So, no. I didn't mean to kill her, and I'm glad she didn't die. I shot to stop her. Now she'll go to trial with a jury of her peers. I hope she goes away for a long time."

"Does it ever bother you? Being a cop, I mean."

She shrugged and sipped her wine. "Sometimes. But it's what I do and I'm good at it. I like helping people. I guess I choose not to overthink it."

He smiled. "I didn't mean to get so heavy. Sorry about that."

"Can I change my answer?" She felt silly for giving such a shallow answer to his earlier question.

"You don't hate olives?"

"Oh, no. I still detest them." She reached for his hand this time. "People who hurt kids. That's something real I really hate."

He nodded and they finished their wine. He asked if she wanted to grab a drink somewhere and maybe find a place to do a little dancing. She wasn't ready for their date to end, so she agreed. He took her to a classy little jazz club downtown and they danced for an hour. It was the perfect, quintessential

70

date. But they both had to work the next day, so as the clock swept toward midnight, he drove her back to Finn and Mel's.

She wondered if he would expect to come in and she wasn't sure what she would say if he seemed inclined. On one hand, she felt completely relaxed and comfortable with him; on the other hand, she was out of her depth with a man like him and not sure what their next steps were. He held her hand as he walked her to the door.

"Do you, um, want to come in?"

He smiled and stepped close. "Of course I do. I'll dream about it all night. But I won't." He cupped her cheek and rubbed his thumb across her skin. "I would like to kiss you goodnight, however. Would that be all right?"

She was amused that he would ask; he hadn't asked earlier in his office. "I think that would be nice."

"I hope it's a notch or two above 'nice.'" He murmured the last word against her lips.

It was. It started soft but quickly deepened as she opened her lips to his hot tongue. He pulled her closer and his hands curved around her bottom. She could feel his arousal pressed against her stomach and was thrilled to know she caused it.

He let her go with a soft groan. "Will you go out with me again, Chrissy? I don't want to play games and wait to call you. I want to date you."

She raised her eyebrows at his honesty. It was refreshing and terrifying. Was she ready to jump into another relationship? She wasn't at all sure, but she stared into his icy blue eyes and nodded. "I'd love to go out with you again."

Chapter Six

Hugh

"Does that feel good?"

"Oh, yes! God, Hugh. Don't stop." She moaned as her head fell back against the sofa cushion.

He grinned and moved to the other foot. "I think I've found your weak spot." He massaged for a few minutes in silence, trying to work the soreness away. "It's been a rough week at work, huh?" She'd been pulling ten hour days and it was starting to catch up with her. They'd gone out the night after their first official date and gotten together after work every night since. For the last few days he'd met her at Finn and Mel's in the evening. He and Bob would stop for take-out or groceries, then head to his brother's house where he would feed Fluff and CJ and wait for Chrissy. They cooked together the first few evenings, but then one of her cases became extremely active, thus her late nights.

"I am beyond ready to get my partner back. Maybe I'll take a couple days off next week." She closed her eyes and slid lower on the sofa. Her feet were propped in Hugh's lap as he rubbed the tension out of them. She'd seemed surprised when he scooped them up and tossed her shoes away. She'd objected, saying they probably reeked, but he didn't care.

"That sounds like a great idea. Finn and Mel get back tomorrow, right?" He let his hands move up past her ankles and began massaging her smooth calves. He loved touching her. He'd let his hands wander a bit more each time they kissed, but wasn't trying to rush her into bed. They were both wary of getting deeply involved in another relationship, and thus didn't want to jump in too soon. For now, he was happy to simply spend time with her.

"Yeah. I'll move back to my apartment around lunchtime. Their plane should get in around one o'clock. Mmm, you have magic hands."

He chuckled and pushed her feet off his lap, reaching for her hands. "I'm glad you think so. Come on. Dinner is ready, and you need to eat before you fall asleep."

"You're spoiling me. How am I ever going to face cereal for dinner again?"

"As long as I'm around, there will be no cereal for dinner, young lady. You deserve a little spoiling." She was such a conundrum: tough talking and fierce as a detective, but soft and feminine as a woman. At least soft in all the right places, as he was discovering. She was also incredibly strong and fit, something he admired. They'd gone running together a couple times in the past week and he'd had to push himself to keep up. "You want to change while I set the table?"

She smiled and put her arms around his neck. "Have I told you how much I appreciate you?"

"Not today. I would be willing to accept any small expressions of gratitude you care to send my way." He pushed her blonde hair behind her ear and smiled into her gray-green eyes.

"You would? Well, let's see what I can do." She placed her lips on his and kissed him sweetly. "Thank you, Hugh."

He rubbed his thumb across her soft lips, then kissed her again. He had to force himself to pull away, knowing she needed food and rest right now more than passion. "My pleasure."

He'd prepared grilled chicken breasts with a basil cream sauce, risotto from a box, and a green salad. He'd found himself perusing the internet earlier that afternoon for recipes he could handle and wondered how in the hell he'd become so domesticated. But then he'd thought of Chrissy and how tired she would be when she got home and shrugged. She was worth it. Besides, it turned out he was a decent cook. He poured them each a glass of the Vinho Verde wine he'd bought after a short conversation he'd struck up with another customer in the wine aisle and felt her arms hug him from behind.

"This looks amazing and smells even better." She kissed the back of his neck, causing shivers of pleasure to streak across his skin.

He set the wine down and turned, swooping in for a quick kiss. "You look beautiful," he said as he held her at arm's length. She'd changed into a greenish-blue sundress and he loved the way it left her shoulders bare. He pulled her chair out and handed her the glass of wine. "Try this."

She sipped and flashed him a half-smile. "It's bubbly. And not too sweet. I love it."

"Good. Me too." He told her how he'd discovered the Portuguese wine and filled her in on the rest of his day, uneventful as it had been. "So, tell me about your day. Did you track down that suspect you mentioned last night?"

"Are you sure you want to hear about police procedurals during dinner? I don't want to bore you to death. This chicken is great, by the way."

"I love hearing about your day. It's never boring. My job is the boring one, except when we're digging up long-dead corpses," he said with a grin.

"I'm glad that doesn't happen too often. It's too damn hard to figure out who they are when they've been dead for three decades." She told him about the case she'd been dealing with for the past week, one which had been on the back burner for months but suddenly heated up when a friend of the number one suspect called with some damning information about the supposed alibi. Without Finn there to help, all the reports and interrogations had fallen on her shoulders. She never complained, but Hugh could see how tired she was.

"How about we curl up on the couch and watch a movie after dinner? Or I can take off if you want to hit the sack early."

"A movie sounds great. I don't want you to leave." She sipped her wine and said softly, "I like spending time with you."

He picked her free hand up from where it lay on the table and kissed the backs of her fingers. "Good, because I like spending time with you too. Listen, my parents are having a welcome back dinner Sunday night for the newlyweds. Will you come with me? It'd be a great time to tell the rest of the family about us, all at once."

"Um, yeah. If you're sure. I don't want to horn in on your family time, though." She appeared adorably unsure.

"I'm positive." He squeezed her hand lightly. "I want to introduce them to my new girlfriend." He watched to see how she reacted. They'd been dating for barely over a week, but he wanted her to know it was exclusive, as far as he was concerned. He was fairly sure she felt the same way, but it was always a risk to blurt it out the first time.

She bit her bottom lip, but smiled. "Your girlfriend, huh? I like the sound of that. So, that makes you my boyfriend. Okay. It's kind of scary, but I like it."

"It *is* kind of scary, but I like it too. Thanks for not freaking out."

She laughed. "No problem. My heart's about to pound out of my chest, though."

"I know what you mean." He joined her laughter, then sobered. "It's been a long time since I've had to go through all the beginning stuff in a relationship. I hope I'm not screwing it up too badly."

"Hey." She reached for his hand. "As far as I can tell, you're doing great. It's been a while for me too. I think we're stumbling through it pretty well. I'm happy."

"Me too, Chrissy." Scared, but happy. She was growing to be extremely important to him, and he feared she was well on the way to becoming integral to his continuing happiness. He had no idea if this was a good idea or not, but he was powerless to stop it. Something about her drew him; it always had, even when they'd first met at Finn's hospital bed. He'd tried valiantly to ignore it for months, but to no avail. He prayed everything worked out, because he didn't think his heart could stand to break again.

She refused to rest while he cleaned up, so they did the dishes together, then settled on the sofa to find a movie. They decided on an old Eddie Murphy flick and Chrissy curled against him to watch. She lasted approximately fifteen minutes before he felt her breathing even out and her head relax against his shoulder. He gently shifted her until she lay with her head pillowed in his lap and let her sleep until the final credits. He considered letting her sleep on the couch while he quietly let himself out, but she woke when he eased out from under her head.

"Mmm. Sorry I fell asleep. I'm not a fun date lately."

"It's not a problem, Chrissy." He kissed her forehead. "Go to bed, sweetheart. I'll lock up."

***

Chris

"You're nervous."

78

"No, of course not." She spoke around her finger, then realized he'd caught her biting her nail. "Maybe a little bit." She clasped her hands in her lap.

"I don't suppose it would help to remind you they already know and love you?" He pulled into the driveway of his parents' house as he asked.

She'd been a guest at the sprawling adobe-style home several times in the past few months and had always thought it lovely, but it now towered above her, menacing and judgmental. "That was before we started dating. They may think differently about me now that I'm your girlfriend." She loved saying it; she still had a hard time believing it, and she wasn't sure how well his family would respond. She dragged herself out of the car and met him in front of the hood.

He took her hand as they walked up the path. "I guarantee they'll like you even better now. You look gorgeous, by the way." They reached the front door, but instead of reaching for the handle, he reached for her, pulling her close. "Don't worry." He whispered the words against her lips.

The door opened and Finn stood, beer in hand, and a grin spreading across his face. "I go away for two weeks and come back to find my big brother and my partner hooking up. What is the world coming to?"

Mel squeezed by him and launched herself into Chris' arms with a squeal. "I'm so excited for you two! Pay no attention to my husband."

Finn laughed and stood aside so they could enter. "I'm glad Hugh finally had the good sense to realize what a catch Chris is. I hate to break it to you, but this," he gestured to Chris and Hugh, holding hands again, "is not exactly a huge surprise."

"Whatever. It's good to see you, Mel." Hugh hugged his new sister-in-law. "Did you have a good time in Hawaii? I hope my idiot brother allowed you to do some sightseeing or go to the beach occasionally."

"Hey!" Finn objected. "Mel's the one who kept me chained to the bed day and night. I was hoping to get a tan, but my wife had other ideas."

Mel blushed and swatted him on the shoulder. "Hush, you! Let's go in. I'm dying to see the look on Cara's face when she sees who Hugh's new girlfriend is."

"Izzy too," Finn said.

"Oh, Izzy knows already. So does Tony," Mel said breezily.

"We've been here ten minutes! How the hell do you know that?" Finn laughed as he slid his arm around his wife.

"I could tell by the gloating look they exchanged when Moira said Hugh was bringing his new mystery girlfriend."

"You're scary sometimes, you know that?" Finn said as he tilted her chin up and kissed her.

The rest of the family was on the back patio, enjoying what would probably be the final weekend of their Indian summer. Cara and Izzy were at the picnic table, fussing over Janey; Seamus and Tony were fetching beer from the cooler; Moira and Big Tony conferenced beside the giant gas grill. Hugh continued to hold her hand as he cleared his throat to get everyone's attention.

"So, Chrissy and I are dating." He turned to her. "You want a beer?"

She glanced at him and rolled her eyes, exasperated. *That's how he decides to tell his family? Seriously?*

Cara gasped and ran to hug Chris. "I can't believe you didn't tell me!" She turned to her brother. "I will get back at you for keeping it a secret! This is so great! You guys are perfect together!"

His mother reacted in a similar, if less effusive, manner. Seamus also said he wasn't surprised and joked that he missed his chance. Hugh's father, Big Tony, smiled widely and asked her how she liked her steak. She had clearly worried for no reason, as Hugh had said. His family seemed to heartily approve of her as his girlfriend. *The last one must have been a nightmare if they're so eager to welcome me.*

When he dropped her off at her apartment later that night, she wondered if he might expect or want to come in, but although he kissed her passionately in the car, running his hands under her blouse and caressing her breasts, he went home after kissing her softly at her door. She watched him drive away, bemused at his reticence. Did he not want to sleep with her? Was she not sending the right signals or something?

***

The next morning, as she worked on a delinquent

report and tried not to obsess over her boyfriend's reluctance to take their relationship to the next level, a barking voice broke the relative silence of the precinct.

"Hart! My office! Now! Bring your partner!" Captain Silva shouted from his office doorway, then ducked back inside.

Chris, startled, dropped her pen and knocked her coffee mug over. "Shit," she muttered and began mopping up. She glanced across the desk at Finn, who grinned and stood, motioning for her to precede him to the captain's office. She entered but stopped short at the sight of the man standing in front the window. His dark blue suit, short haircut, and general demeanor screamed 'Fed.'

"Hart, DeLuca, this is Special Agent Daniels with the FBI. He's here about the bodies found at the construction site."

She and Finn shook hands with the man, but she wondered what on earth the FBI wanted with a local body dump case. How did they even find out? They'd managed to keep it out of the local media, so there was no buzz about it.

The captain spoke from behind his desk. "Your bullet fragments have raised some interest with the FBI."

"How so?" Chris sat in one of the chairs in front of his desk.

Agent Daniels spoke up. "One of the fragments has raised our interest. I don't have any information about the other five."

"Sir?" Chris addressed the captain.

He pulled a sheet of paper from a manila folder

and handed it to her. "This is the ballistics report. It came in this morning. Agent Daniels arrived a few minutes later. The bullets in five of the bodies were fired from the same gun, a .357 Magnum Colt revolver made in the late 1960s."

"But I'm here to talk about the bullet from the sixth body." Agent Daniels crossed the room to sit in the other chair in front Captain Silva's desk, leaned back and continued. "It's from a .38 Special Smith & Wesson Model 13. It's the sidearm FBI agents typically carried in the late 70s and early 80s. That particular weapon was registered to Special Agent Thomas Barilla, who has been missing since January 12, 1982. He disappeared while working undercover to expose a crime syndicate in New Mexico. It appears you may have discovered where he ended up."

"Holy shit, this was a mob hit?" Chris was floored.

"It's starting to look like it," Silva said. "Have you briefed DeLuca yet?"

"Yes, sir."

"Good. Looks like you got back just in time for a real shit show, DeLuca. We're cooperating with the FBI on this one, so I expect you two to play nice with Agent Daniels and anyone else he brings in. Got it? This will not become a pissing contest."

"Yes, sir," Finn and Chris spoke in unison.

"Good. Why don't you find Daniels a desk and get to work figuring out what the hell we're dealing with? I can't keep it from the media much longer. Goddamn reporters…" They could hear him muttering as they left the office.

Finn found an empty desk in the corner and moved it adjacent to theirs. Chris was glad to see his limp was less pronounced than it had been a few weeks ago. The doctors had assured him his ankle would eventually heal to be nearly as good as new, but it was a long, painful road.

Agent Daniels made himself at home, leaning back and propping his ankle on his knee. Chris took note of his short blond curls, tan skin, even white teeth; he looked like he'd be more at home on a surfboard than in his bland FBI-approved suit. He should have taken up modeling. She'd bet her next paycheck he had a great body under those professional layers. Not that she had any desire to know, of course. She was perfectly happy with her boyfriend's body. Or she was sure she would be, if she ever got the opportunity to see it.

"Would you like to read the report I've been working on?" she asked.

"Yes, thanks." He flashed her a crooked grin as she handed him the file.

"Would you like some coffee or something? It's terrible, but…" She shrugged, wondering why she felt awkward around the man.

"Sure, Lieutenant Hart. One sugar, no cream, please." He smiled at her again, then turned his attention to the report.

She raised her eyebrows. Lieutenant? He'd apparently looked her up. She crossed to the coffee station, Finn at her heels.

"I don't like him."

She poured a cup of the swill that passed for coffee at the station, added a sugar packet, and turned to her partner. "Are you worried he's going to take the title of Best-Looking Cop in the Precinct from you?"

"You're hilarious, Chris. Really." He reached past her to pour himself a refill. "He's too smarmy for my taste, that's all."

"I'll reserve judgment for the time being. We need to get along with him. So, the FBI is involved in this. Interesting."

"And it looks like we're about to get a crash course in mafia dealings in New Mexico. I can hardly wait."

She led the way back to their desks and handed Daniels his coffee.

"Thanks." He winked at her over the rim of the mug.

She felt Finn nudge her from behind and turned to glower at him before turning back to the FBI agent. "So, how about you tell us what *you* know? You've got our report, so you know everything *we* know."

"Sort of a *quid pro quo*?"

"If you like." Chris was starting to see what Finn meant. "Listen, we've been told to cooperate with you, and we're trying. We need each other's help—"

He pushed away from his desk and stood. "Actually, Lieutenants." He gestured to both Finn and Chris. "You were told to cooperate with me. I wasn't given quite the same directive." He took a sip of the awful coffee and set the mug on the desk. "Thanks for the coffee, Lt. Hart. I'll bring this report back real soon."

They watched him leave and Finn huffed out a harsh laugh. "So long, Agent Douchebag. Nice meeting you. Now what?" He addressed the last words to Chris.

"Now we start investigating."

"With what to go on? Agent Dickhead didn't share with the class, if you remember."

"We've got a name, and we know it has something to do with mob activity in Albuquerque. We can start there," Chris said.

"Mob activity from more than thirty years ago," Finn objected.

Chris grinned at him. "It certainly makes it more of a challenge, huh? How's your aim, Finn?"

"My aim?"

"Yeah. This just turned into a pissing contest."

Chapter Seven

Hugh

Okay. So, Chrissy and I are dating. Good, good. But now what? He sat at his desk, staring at his computer screen, wondering what in the world he was supposed to do next. He should be putting together a bid for a new job, but he couldn't focus. It had been a long time—too long—since he'd had to think about dating. He and Lauren had been together so long he'd forgotten how to start a new relationship. He tried to remember what he'd done when he'd first met Lauren, how he'd wooed her, how he'd let her know how special she was, and how interested he was. She'd recently finished law school and was working for a large law firm when they'd met at a party hosted by one of his commercial clients. He was still working for his dad, but Big Tony had announced his intentions to retire within the year. Hugh had been floored by the beauty of the young lawyer and set out to impress her with whatever wit and charm he could muster. Much to his surprise, she'd given him her phone number at the end of the party and had actually agreed to go out with him. He struggled to remember what he'd done, anything particular he'd said. God, he didn't remember it being so difficult. Then again, he'd been a lot younger and a heck of a lot more naïve back then. He'd had no idea how quickly love could turn to hate. Betrayal did that to a person. Ugh! He sunk his head onto his arms. Reflecting on his failed relationship with Lauren was giving him a headache, and it wasn't helping him figure out how to move his relationship with Chrissy forward.

"Well, well, well." Cara waltzed into his office. She never bothered with something as polite as knocking. "Catching up on your sleep? Chris must be keeping you up very, very late. All night, in fact." She wiggled her eyebrows up and down.

I wish. But he couldn't seem to get quite to the point of asking her to stay the night. He wanted to, of course, but it would take their relationship to a level he wasn't sure they were ready for. *I'm not sure I'm ready for that.* He could at least be honest with himself. Sleeping with her meant they were serious, at least in his mind. He'd never been one for casual sex, and he didn't plan to start now. "Did you need something, Cara?"

"Ooh, someone's a grumpy bear this morning! Maybe I'll have a word with Chris and let her know you need more sleep at your advanced age. She should take it easy on you." Cara folded herself gracefully onto the sofa, a look of mock concern on her beautiful face.

"Is there a reason you're gracing me with your presence this morning? Did you get fired from your teaching job?"

"Yes, I'd love a cup of coffee, Big Brother. Thanks so much." She raised her eyebrows expectantly until he rose and poured her a cup. "It's a three-day weekend. I have one glorious day off from teaching hormonal teenagers. I'm stealing Izzy away for a few hours. I hope you don't mind."

"Would it even begin to matter if I did? So, why am I blessed with your lounging ass on my sofa if you came for Izzy?" His words were cranky but his tone was even; he'd always had a soft spot for his little sister. He still remembered his first sight of the tiny baby his mother had placed in his arms when he was seven years old. She was red, wrinkled, and adorable. She'd stolen his heart completely and he'd never quite gotten past it. She'd always been able to manipulate him into doing pretty much whatever she wanted. Her divorce five years ago had nearly wrecked him; how could he not have known her marriage was on the rocks? Was he so out of touch with his beloved little sister he missed what was going on right under his nose?

"I wanted to see you, Hugh! Is that a crime?"

He narrowed his eyes at her.

"Fine. I want to hear all about you and Chris. I can't believe you told Izzy and Tony before me!" She leaned close and swatted him on the arm.

"Calm down. I didn't tell anyone. Tony showed up uninvited when Chrissy was there. Izzy busted in here when Chrissy stopped by to talk about the investigation."

"Yeah, that's what they said. I guess I'll forgive you." She sipped her coffee silently. "I'm really glad, Hugh." She was serious for a moment, reaching out to touch his hand. "You deserve to be happy. She's really great."

"You deserve it too, Cara." He squeezed her hand and then smiled. "She is great. I'm not exactly sure I know what I'm doing. It's been a while." He sighed and stood, crossing his office to pace in front of the window.

"Hey." She set her coffee on the table and crossed the room to hug him. "Looks to me like you're doing fine. I've never seen her smile so much. What are you worried about?"

He had no intention of discussing his sex life, or lack thereof, with his little sister. "It's been a while since I've had to think about planning dates and that sort of thing."

"I wouldn't worry about it too much. Chris has had a crush on you for months. I'm sure she'll be thrilled with whatever you do."

"She had a crush on me? She told you that?" He was flabbergasted. He'd thought he'd been the only one struggling with infatuation.

"No, she didn't say anything. She didn't have to. I have eyes. I watched the way she undressed you with hers every time you came around—"

"Shut up." He sighed and ran his hands through his hair. "Do I hear Izzy calling you?"

She laughed. "You wish." She finished the last sip of her coffee and stood. "All right. I'm going." She reached up on tiptoe to kiss him on the cheek.

"Try not to worry, Hugh. You and Chrissy are perfect together. See you later."

He smiled crookedly as she sailed out the door to steal his business partner away for the rest of the day, most likely. He returned to his desk to finish the bid he'd been working on when Cara interrupted. If he could make himself get some damn work done, he might be able to steal an hour or two and stop by to visit with Chrissy. If he was very lucky he'd talk her into going out to lunch with him. He could use the excuse of needing to check in with her about his construction site and when he might be able to re-open it. He rolled his eyes at his own ridiculousness; why in the world did he need an excuse to see his girlfriend?

He immersed himself in work for a few hours, even managing to set up a meeting with an elusive client for a contract he'd been trying to land for several months. It was close to noon when he closed his laptop and stretched. He stopped by his secretary's desk on the way out.

"Malva, would you get this preliminary contract for Gerald Santiago put together this afternoon, please? I just set up a meeting with him for early next week."

"Of course, Hugh. Will you be back this afternoon?"

"I don't think so. I doubt Izzy will, either. Why don't you go home a couple hours early since it's Friday?"

"Thanks. I may take you up on that." She smiled at him as he left.

He wanted to take Chrissy something. Flowers?

Classic, but it might embarrass her to receive flowers at the precinct this early in their relationship. Chocolate? She had a sweet tooth, so he decided to pick up a couple of good chocolate bars for her to keep in her desk.

When he arrived at the low, brick building it was past noon. The receptionist waved him back and he found Finn at his desk, but no Chrissy.

"She's in with the ADA. What's in the bag?" Finn asked.

"A gift for Chrissy. What's the ADA?"

"Assistant district attorney. I was busy questioning a witness, so she's handling it. It's apparently a new guy from the District Attorney's office assigned to one of the cases Chris worked on while I was gone. She should be finished in a few minutes. What, no gift for your brother? Sheesh! I see how it is."

"I doubt it. You mind if I wait for her?"

Finn motioned for him to sit in the chair next to his desk. "You want to grab some lunch?"

"Um, I was kind of hoping to take Chrissy. Alone. You don't mind, do you?" He didn't particularly want to piss his brother off, but he wanted to spend time with his girlfriend.

Finn smirked. "A little 'afternoon delight,' huh? Good idea. Maybe I'll go home for lunch and see if my beautiful wife is amenable."

Hugh rolled his eyes and both men chuckled. Voices from the back of the room interrupted them and Hugh turned to see Chrissy walking out of a conference room with a petite brunette Hugh assumed must be the assistant district attorney. He smiled as he watched Chrissy walk toward him, smiling at something the woman said. His stomach clenched as the woman turned and he realized he knew her. He knew her well, in fact. It was Lauren, his ex.

***

Chrissy

She'd enjoyed meeting the new ADA; the woman seemed sensible, smart, and down to earth. Chris found herself eyeing the petite woman's dress and heels with envy; she'd love to be able to wear something like that to work, but her job demanded clothing that could stand up to all kinds of situations, therefore she was limited to sensible pants and sturdy shoes. She never knew when she'd be walking through mud, shit, or even chasing down a suspect. This woman, Lauren Babcock, was gorgeous, and made Chris feel frumpy and large in her khakis and button down shirt, but she was also extremely nice and Chris looked forward to working with her.

They chatted as they crossed the room and Chris glanced up to see Hugh sitting with Finn. What a sweet guy he was to stop by to surprise her. She smiled at her boyfriend, but he didn't return it. In fact, he didn't seem to notice her at all. She frowned and tried to determine what had claimed his attention so completely. He was staring at the ADA, a frown on his face. Lauren turned to see what had captured Chris's attention and froze when she saw

Hugh. Chris could feel the sudden tension in the room. What was going on here?

"Hugh." Lauren breathed the name.

He stood as they approached. "Lauren." His voice was colder than Chris had ever heard it, causing the hair on her neck to stand up. He didn't even glance her way. She could see the muscles in his jaw clenching.

"Oh, shit," Finn murmured.

Hugh turned to look at his brother.

"I didn't know, Hugh. I swear."

Hugh sighed and looked back at Lauren. He still hadn't acknowledged Chris. "So, you made it to the district attorney's office, huh? Well, congratulations. I know how important that was to you." He spat the words out.

Chris cast about in her mind for some rhyme or reason for the venom in his voice when it suddenly struck her: this must be his ex-girlfriend. Oh, great. Perfect. She already felt dowdy in comparison to the woman and that was before she knew Hugh had slept with her for years. She wanted to disappear.

"Yes, it was important to me," Lauren replied, her tone defensive. "I never lied about that, Hugh."

"No, lying was never your problem, Lauren." He huffed out a harsh chuckle and rubbed his hand over his face. "Shit. I did not need this today." He finally turned to Chris. "I'm sorry. I'll call you later, okay?" He handed her the small paper bag he'd been holding and left quickly.

"Well, that was awkward," Finn said as the door shut behind his brother.

Lauren sighed and turned to him. "Hello, Finn. I

didn't expect to run into you here. I figured you'd be out on patrol."

"I'm a detective now. I spend a lot more time chained to my desk these days."

"Congratulations. I was really sorry to hear about your accident."

Chris realized the two of them must have spent quite a lot of time together over the years. It made her feel like even more of a third wheel.

"Thanks, Lauren. I'm doing a lot better now. Did you hear I got married?"

"No! Wow, that's great." She turned to Chris. "Is this your—"

"No, I'm just his partner," she cut in quickly. She didn't know how to act. Hugh obviously had issues with the woman and loyalty to him had Chris reversing her earlier friendliness.

Finn seemed to understand her conundrum and broke in easily. "My wife's name is Melanie. She's a writer and graphic designer."

"Well, that's great." She looked hard at Chris, a frown line between her eyebrows. "Are you and Hugh dating?" She shook her head. "Sorry. It's none of my business—"

"We are." Chris said it flatly; Lauren could take it or leave it.

She smiled briefly. "Good. He deserves someone nice. He's a good man." She shook her head again and shouldered her large bag. "I should get back to my office. It was nice to meet you, Chris. Take care, Finn." She nodded briefly at both and left.

"She's Hugh's ex," Chris stated flatly.

"Yep." He must have realized she was bothered

by this revelation. "Listen, Chris. They broke up over a year ago. Hugh isn't carrying a torch for her or anything, so don't worry."

Then why was he so upset by seeing her again? Maybe it had something to do with the fact they had been engaged, which Finn didn't know. She realized seeing an ex unexpectedly totally sucked, but his reaction had been extreme. She tried to understand, but was incredibly hurt by his dismissal of her. He'd barely acknowledged her, much less introduced her as his new girlfriend. Was he comparing her—unfavorably—to his old flame? She didn't care for the feelings this thought engendered, so she waved Finn's assurances away and moved to sit at her desk. She certainly didn't want to discuss it with her partner, who also happened to be her boyfriend's brother. The paper bag was still in her hand and she finally peered inside to find three large chocolate bars from Trader Joe's. He'd stopped to pick up a small present for her. What was she supposed to feel? She was hurt by his callous treatment, but touched by his remembrance and unplanned visit. Had he planned to ask her to lunch? She opened her top drawer and set the chocolate inside; she couldn't process this right now. Tears were trying to push their way out of her eyes and she couldn't allow it. She sniffed and slammed the drawer shut. She glanced up to see Finn staring at her.

"What?" she demanded, then felt bad for how harsh and bitchy she sounded.

"Nothing." He started shuffling papers on his desk, refusing to meet her glare.

"Good. Let's get back to work." She sorted through the piles on her own desk. "Goddammit! Have you seen the Baker file?"

He silently handed her the file from his desk.

For the first time in her career, she was glad to be buried in paperwork and reports for the rest of the afternoon. She focused her attention on her computer screen, barely acknowledging Finn when he left for lunch. She hoped he knew enough to keep his mouth shut about the episode, but she wouldn't be terribly surprised if Mel, Cara, and Izzy all knew about it within the hour. Shit.

She placed her cell phone on her desk and checked it all afternoon, half-expecting, half-hoping for a text from Hugh. There was nothing. At four, she straightened the files and grabbed her purse. "I'm going home. I worked through lunch."

"No problem," Finn said quickly. "Have a good weekend."

Once home, she couldn't seem to settle to anything. She started to clean her apartment, but she spent more time checking her phone. He didn't call or text. She fixed herself a sandwich, but wasn't remotely hungry and ended up throwing most of it away. *God, snap out of it, girl! He's just a guy and not worth all this angst!* But she didn't believe her self-talk. Hugh wasn't simply another guy. He was amazing, and she thought they had a shot at something special. But how could she compete against his gorgeous ex-girlfriend? And was it even a competition? She didn't know what had happened between them, but his reaction earlier had been more anger than anything else. He was furious with

97

Lauren for some reason. But why hadn't he called?

She managed to make a pretense of staying busy until close to six o'clock, when she decided a long run would be the best way to work off this funk. He still hadn't made contact. She stepped outside in her shorts and t-shirt and realized the temperature had dropped dramatically since she'd left work. She glanced toward the west mesa and realized a storm was moving in, the clouds black and threatening in the gathering dusk. But Albuquerque weather could change on a dime, so even if it rained it would likely be a quick shower. She shivered and realized the beautiful Indian summer was apparently at an end. She thought about going back inside for a sweatshirt, but decided she'd probably end up taking it off halfway through her run as she got sweaty.

Two miles later she felt the first chilly drops. She determinedly ignored the precipitation and ran harder. Another mile and the heavens opened up, drenching her to the skin within minutes. *Shit. Fuck. Why didn't I bring my goddamn cell phone?* She looked around to see where she was and realized Hugh's house was less than a quarter of a mile away. She had paid little attention to where she was running, but her subconscious had apparently led her to him. She shrugged and pushed her wet hair out of her face. *Well, I'll at least find out what the hell is going on.* She shivered and continued running.

Chapter Eight

Hugh

Christ, what a day. Hugh poured himself another two fingers of bourbon and tried to decide if he could muster the energy to order a pizza. His head still pounded, although he'd downed three aspirin when he got home. *All I wanted was to stop by and surprise my girlfriend. I never expected to see Lauren.* The thought of her and what she'd done sent his stomach into a nauseated roll. *No pizza. Definitely not.* He sipped the alcohol, hissing as it burned its way down his throat. He was well on his way to a roaring drunk, something he hadn't done in over a year. Since he and Lauren had called it quits, to be exact. But seeing her again had brought it all back. And, oh yeah, he'd treated Chrissy like shit. He'd only had eyes for her as she walked out of the conference room, looking so cute and badass with her gun and shoulder holster, and he'd hoped he could lure her away for lunch and maybe a fair amount of kissing in the cab of his truck. Finn's "afternoon delight" comment had brought up all sorts of delicious ideas. Then the shorter woman walking with her had turned, and all those wonderful thoughts had evaporated as a haze of anger had taken their place. He tried to remember if he'd even acknowledged Chrissy's presence, but feared he hadn't. He knew he should call her, but he had no idea what he could possibly say. *God, if I've screwed this up, I don't know what I'm going to do.* He was still beyond furious with Lauren, and he knew it was time to move on, but he was afraid. He'd put everything into his relationship with Lauren, assuming it would eventually turn into marriage and a family. But it hadn't. It definitely hadn't. He didn't know if he was ready to go there again. He'd begun the relationship with Chrissy hoping it could be simple…temporary. But he already knew it was much more than that. She was special and she deserved someone who knew it and acted on it. He feared he couldn't be that man. An especially loud crack of thunder struck nearby, causing Bob to whimper and lean his furry body against Hugh's leg. The storm raging outside felt appropriate, mirroring the turmoil roiling inside him.

The doorbell and Bob's resulting bark interrupted his increasingly depressing thoughts. Crap. Which one of his well-meaning siblings would he have to get rid of? Finn had undoubtedly spread the word of his encounter with his ex. If he didn't answer, maybe whichever one it was would assume he was out and would leave. He sipped his drink and hoped. The doorbell rang again, followed by several knocks, and he forced himself off the sofa. He'd lay odds it was Seamus, although it was nearly as likely to be Cara. He peered through the peephole and discovered it was neither.

"Christ," he muttered and wrenched the door open. "Are you crazy? It's pouring out there and you still went for a run?" He pulled a sopping wet, shivering Chrissy inside, where she dripped all over the tile in his entryway.

"Yeah, well, it wasn't raining when I left," she said through chattering teeth.

"You're lucky you weren't struck by lightning! I can't believe you ran all the way over here." Her arms were covered in gooseflesh and she looked miserable.

"I'm sorry to bother you, Hugh, but I didn't bring my cell phone. Could I maybe borrow a towel? I'm sure it will clear up in a few minutes and I can head home." As if in answer, another huge crack of thunder exploded, startling her.

"Jesus, Chrissy," he said on a sigh. "Come on." He grabbed her hand and towed her upstairs to his bedroom and into the large master bath. "Take a hot shower and get warmed up. Just leave your wet clothes on the floor and I'll put them in the dryer. There's a robe on the back of the door you can wear while they're drying. I'll make coffee and meet you downstairs when you're done, okay?"

She simply nodded and stepped past him into the bathroom.

He shut the door and waited until he heard the shower start. He shook his head and headed downstairs to make coffee so she'd have something hot to drink when she got done with her shower. Once the coffee maker was going, he raced back upstairs and knocked on the bathroom door before opening it slightly and reaching in for her sopping clothes. He caught a glimpse of her long, lean, and wonderfully naked body through the steamy glass of the shower door and made himself look away. *Sex is surely the last thing on her mind right now, idiot! She's frozen half to death. Plus, she may not even be speaking to you after the way you treated her earlier today.*

When she came downstairs wearing his robe, her hair wet and mussed, he had a steaming mug of coffee waiting for her on the table in front of the sofa. She sat, curling her long legs beneath her, and reached for it. She took a sip and groaned with pleasure; the sound went straight to Hugh's gut and regions a bit lower.

"This tastes like more whiskey than coffee," she murmured over the top of the mug.

"I figured you could use it."

She smiled and took another sip. "Thanks. I'm finally warming up. It sure got cold suddenly, huh?"

They were going to talk about the weather? "Yeah. Looks like it's finally fall." He sipped his own coffee, which he had switched to—sans whiskey—while she was in the shower. "Chrissy, I'm sorry."

"For what?"

"For not calling."

"Oh that."

"Yeah, that." He hated this sudden awkwardness between them, hated knowing he'd caused it by his cavalier treatment of her. "Lauren Babcock is my ex-girlfriend. My ex-fiancée. I didn't expect to see her today and it threw me."

"I'll say." She drank her coffee for several moments as the silence stretched between them. "You looked so angry, Hugh. What did she do? Did she cheat on you? Is that why you're so mad at her?"

He sighed and shook his head. He absolutely didn't want to have this conversation, but he owed it to her. If he had any hope of smoothing things over with her, he had to explain. And it was important to him to get their relationship back on track and moving forward. "No, she didn't cheat. Shit." He stood and began pacing. "Listen, I need to explain, or try to anyway, but it's still hard to talk about."

She bit her lip, but nodded encouragingly. "I'll try to understand. It's coming between us right now and I need to know if you and I are going to work. I need to know if you want us to work."

"You're right." He ran his hands through his hair, making a mess out of it but not caring. "I do want us to work, Chrissy. It's really important to me. You're important to me." He stopped in front of her and reached to cup her cheek briefly and run his thumb over her smooth lips, then resumed his pacing. "Lauren and I were together for five years. I met her soon after she graduated from law school, and we hit it off right away. I knew from the beginning how important her career was to her. At least I thought I did. I thought we could still have a life together: marriage, a couple kids, a house, a dog. I asked her to marry me the first time two years into our relationship. She didn't say 'no' outright. She said 'not yet'. She kept saying it for three more years, but I loved her and never gave up hoping I could change her mind. She always had something she wanted to do first: get hired by a top law firm, make more money, make it to the district attorney's office. I was blind, I guess, and couldn't see what was right in front of my face." He laughed ruefully. "She had no intention of marrying me. She was perfectly happy with the way things were. She had her own place, but stayed over at mine frequently. I had a condo back then." He shook his head at his inclusion of this seemingly unimportant detail. "Then she got pregnant."

Chrissy sucked in an audible breath and set her mug on the table. "You have a child with her, Hugh? How come—"

"No." He stopped pacing and flopped on the sofa next to her. "When I found out, I was ecstatic. I proposed yet again, and this time she actually said yes. I practically dragged her to the jewelry store and bought her the biggest engagement ring I could afford. I wanted her to move in and she said she would. Everything was perfect."

"What happened?" She placed her hand on his arm and he was glad to feel it was warm.

He covered her hand with his own and linked their fingers. "A few days after she told me about the baby, she came home from work and told me she'd had an abortion earlier that afternoon."

"You're fucking kidding me!"

"Nope. She was so calm. She handed back the engagement ring and said she wasn't ready for marriage and a family, so she'd 'taken care' of the problem. She called our baby a problem." He finished on a whisper and was horrified to feel the damn tears pressing behind his eyes. He sniffed, trying to control his emotions.

"Oh, my God," Chrissy whispered. Then she let go of his hand and scooted closer, slipping her arms around his waist and resting her head against his shoulder. "I'm so sorry, Hugh."

He rested his head on top of hers and swallowed the giant lump in his throat. Her body was warm, and she smelled so damn good. He put his arm around her and held her close, accepting the gift of comfort she offered. "Thank you. None of my family knows. I'd rather they didn't. My mom would be devastated." He held her several more moments. "I'm really sorry about how I behaved earlier. I just didn't know what to say to you. Seeing Lauren brought it all back." He pulled back and looked into her beautiful gray-green eyes. He was fascinated by how they changed color, more gray tonight than he'd ever seen them. "I care about you, Chrissy. I care a lot, but I'm scared. I don't know if I'm ready for another serious relationship yet, and this feels serious."

She smiled crookedly and reached to smooth his hair. "I know, and it scares the shit out of me too. I don't suppose there's any way we could agree to take it one day at a time? Maybe not overthink it?"

The huge knot in his gut relaxed ever so slightly. She seemed to understand, at least somewhat. "Yeah, that sounds good." He leaned in and kissed her softly, savoring the lingering taste of coffee and whiskey. "Your clothes are probably dry. You can change and then I'll drive you home." He started to stand.

She held on to his hand and pulled his head back down for another kiss, this one searing and deep. "What if I don't want to go home?" she whispered, staring into his eyes and biting her lip, as if she was afraid of his answer.

He knew what she was asking, and he wanted it with every fiber of his being. God, of course he wanted it, wanted her. But still he hesitated. "Are you sure?"

She smiled in answer and shifted herself to sit on his lap. She wrapped her arms around his neck and leaned in to kiss his jaw, working her way up to nibble at his earlobe, her tongue darting out to soothe where her teeth had been. "Positive."

***

Chrissy

She awoke to a very wet tongue slurping across her face. She blinked her eyes open and found herself staring into a pair of soulful brown ones. She smiled and reached a hand from under the covers to stroke Bob's soft golden head. He whimpered and placed a paw on the bed.

"Don't even think about it, buddy." Hugh's voice was a low, sleepy growl behind her.

She rolled over carefully and saw he was awake, but barely. "Does he need to go out?"

Hugh mumbled something unintelligible and

pulled her close, tucking her head under his chin.

She went willingly and smiled when she felt the bed give way as Bob took her place. She heard Hugh mutter something that sounded like 'damn dog.' "Good morning." She whispered the words against his naked chest and followed them with a kiss. The night before had been something of a revelation to Chris, as Hugh had taken her to heights previously unknown in her limited sexual experience. Her first serious boyfriend in college hadn't had a clue how to do more than the bare minimum in bed, but she hadn't known any better either. There had been a couple of short-term boyfriends in between him and her last relationship, a long-term live-in boyfriend, with whom she'd shared an active sex life; she now realized it had been fairly tame compared with what Hugh offered and expected in bed. Or on the couch. They hadn't exactly made it to the bedroom last night after she moved to sit on his lap. Once he'd realized she was serious about wanting to be with him, he'd had the robe off her in less than thirty seconds and had begun learning what brought her pleasure. Intense pleasure. Twice, in fact, before he'd even removed his own clothing, retrieved a condom from his wallet, and brought her on top of him to take him deeply inside. It had felt so incredible—being touched and held again after two years—she'd closed her eyes and thrown her head back to just feel. But Hugh insisted she look at him as he urged her back up to the heights of another, even more intense climax before he let himself find release. Once they'd recovered, she wondered if she should offer to leave, but before she could speak, he'd gently lifted her from his lap and kissed her softly, apologizing for rushing though their first time. Then he'd taken her hand and led her upstairs to his bedroom, where he'd demonstrated his diverse talents, making slow, sweet love to her. She'd always feared she wasn't good at the whole sex-thing because she'd never found much satisfaction in it, but with Hugh it was an entirely different story. He was a demanding lover, asking what she liked, and finding with unerring accuracy the places which brought her the most pleasure. He also wasn't shy about telling her what he liked and how he wanted to be touched and tasted. He'd poured himself into her three more times between short naps and, cuddled close against him this morning, she could feel he wanted her again. She smiled and reached down to stroke him, letting him know she was more than amenable.

"As amazing as that feels, angel, I think I should feed you first. I didn't exactly offer you any food last night before my mind was on other things for the rest of the night."

She laughed and brought her hand up to cup his cheek, loving the scratchy feel of his night's growth of whiskers. He had a heavy, dark beard, and looked rather rakish in the dim morning light. She'd only ever seen him clean shaven and smooth and she realized he probably shaved in the evening before their dates. "Can you hear my stomach growling?"

"It's either yours or Bob's. That's why he's up here nagging us to get up. He has a doggy door, but he hasn't mastered getting his own kibble yet. I keep working on it, but his lack of opposable thumbs is presenting a challenge."

She laughed again and traced the crinkles at the corner of his eye as he grinned. *I'm falling in love with him.* Her laughter ceased abruptly with the realization. *Slow down, girl! You had sex with him and, yeah, it was great, but love? Too fast, too much.* She retracted her hand and turned to get out of his bed, searching the floor fruitlessly for her clothes or even the robe. She had a regrettable tendency to fall too fast, too hard into her relationships and she was determined not to make the same mistake this time.

He noticed her sudden change of emotion and crossed the room, unashamedly naked, and pulled her against his strong body, tilting her chin up and looking intently into her face. His ice blue eyes saw entirely too much. "Hey. What's wrong?"

She tried to smile but failed. "Nothing. I'm fine. And starving, but I can't seem to find anything to wear."

He raised an eyebrow, clearly realizing she wasn't being entirely forthcoming but seeming to accept her need to keep some things to herself for the moment. "Okay," he said as he nodded slowly. "Good thing it's a clothing-optional breakfast." He tweaked her nose and let her go, crossing to his closet. He reached inside and grabbed one of his button-up shirts. "Here. You can fulfill another one of my fantasies by wearing this to breakfast."

She chuckled and put it on, rolling up the sleeves while she watched his muscled backside disappear into a pair of jeans. God, he was gorgeous with a chiseled, olive-toned chest and abdomen lightly sprinkled with dark hair, which disappeared enticingly into the waistband of his jeans. He pulled on a t-shirt, called to Bob, and left the room, telling her to come down when she was ready. She finished buttoning his shirt—it was so weird that guy's shirts buttoned the wrong way—and sank back onto his bed. *Okay, calm down. You can't help how you feel, but you don't have to blab to him. He certainly doesn't need or want to know this early in your relationship. You'll likely scare him off after what he's been through with Lauren.* When he'd told her what Lauren had done, how she'd had an abortion without even warning him, her heart had hurt for him. Oh, she knew the whole "my body, my choice" bit, and part of her even agreed with it, but Lauren had been in a loving, committed relationship. She hadn't given Hugh a chance to disagree or try to change her mind. Knowing him, he would have gladly agreed to raise the child himself rather than have her abort it. Lauren had taken matters into her own hands, completely disregarding Hugh's desires. What. A. Bitch.

She shook off her melancholy thoughts and went downstairs, following the alluring aroma of bacon. "What can I do to help?"

"I got this. Coffee's ready. Mugs are above the microwave." He turned the bacon and began cracking eggs into a bowl.

She poured herself a mug and leaned against the counter to watch him cook. Bob sat close by, no doubt hoping Hugh would drop some bacon. "You're quite a catch, Mr. DeLuca."

"Oh? How so?" He didn't turn from his chore.

"World-class sex and a hot breakfast. Wow."

He laughed and continued beating the eggs. "World-class, huh? I think I'm blushing."

"I doubt it." She crossed the room and put one arm around him as she stared into the pans on the stove. "That looks delicious."

"I'm not a great cook, but I get by. And you didn't have dinner last night, so I don't think you'll be terribly discriminating." He leaned down and kissed her quickly. "Last night was amazing for me too, Chrissy. I'm so glad you ran over to my house. I hope you'll run over here often."

She laughed and kissed him before returning to her coffee. "I might even drive occasionally." Being with him made her happy, she realized. She'd been devastated by his coldness in the wake of Lauren's visit, but now that she understood and they were back on track with their relationship, she felt joy infusing every corner of her being. She hugged those feelings to herself and concentrated on the plate of steaming food he placed in front of her. He'd cooked the bacon perfectly—not too crisp— and the eggs were fluffy and light. She waved away the jar of salsa and watched, amused, as he slathered it over his own eggs.

"So," he said around a mouthful, "what have you got going on today? Do you have to work?"

"Nope. Being a detective is a Monday through Friday gig for the most part. Why? What do you have in mind?"

"Nothing specific, but I was hoping we could spend it together."

"I'd like that. I need to grab a quick shower and stop by my place to pick up some clothes, if you don't mind." She stood to fetch them each more coffee.

"Thanks," he said and reached for her hand across the table. "I'd be happy to show you the finer points of my shower right after breakfast. I'm sure there are a few features you didn't notice last night."

She giggled—she couldn't remember the last time she'd done that—and squeezed his hand. "I'm sure that would be a big help."

It was, in that he showed her how to adjust the dual shower heads. She was grateful for his apparently huge hot water heater, as it was a rather lengthy shower. She was also grateful for how large the shower was, capable of allowing two large adults to indulge in all sorts of fun things without once cracking an elbow or knee on the hard tile. She'd never been a huge fan of shower sex before, but she'd clearly been doing it in the wrong shower and definitely with the wrong guy. Her fears that her responsiveness and sensuality of the night before had been a fluke were soundly put to rest over the course of the weekend spent with Hugh. They didn't spend all their time in bed. They went to lunch after stopping by her apartment to pick up extra clothes. He convinced her to bring enough for the whole weekend, plus work clothes for Monday morning and she happily complied.

They met Finn and Mel for dinner Saturday night and spent a few enjoyable hours with the other couple. It was clear Hugh and Finn were close

112

friends as well as brothers, and she enjoyed getting to know Mel without Cara or Izzy there. She loved both the other women, but Mel was quiet and easily overshadowed, by Cara's personality, especially. But, although she was introverted, she wasn't shy. She had a great sense of humor and was highly intelligent, able to speak knowledgeably on a wide range of topics, which elevated the conversation and made for a memorable evening. Sunday was spent lounging in bed, making love, reading the paper, making love, eating a late brunch, making love, napping, and making love again before heading to his parents' house for dinner. Seamus brought his girlfriend and she made everyone uncomfortable by conspicuously refusing to eat anything with carbs. He thankfully took her home early and the rest of the family visibly relaxed in her absence. Hugh spent a half hour sitting on the floor with Janey, playing Memory, while Chris, Izzy, Mel, and Cara did the dishes and cleaned up the kitchen, refusing to let Moira help. It was her second Sunday with his family as his girlfriend and she was gratified by how quickly they accepted her.

They were seated on the sofa Sunday night, watching the news and trying to make the most of their last night together before the world intruded the next morning with work. She had her feet in Hugh's lap and was nearly distracted by his rough hands rubbing and sliding higher and higher with each pass, when a story on the television grabbed her attention. She swung her legs off his lap and snatched the remote to turn the volume up.

"The FBI is cooperating fully with local law

enforcement, but we want to reiterate that this is not something the public needs to be concerned with. The bodies are several decades old. It is not thought to be the work of a serial killer at this point in time." The name below the man talking on screen was FBI Special Agent Jared Daniels. The man himself managed to look like he was posing for a spread in *GQ,* with his tan face and blond hair.

"Son of a bitch," she muttered.

"That's my job site! How the hell did they get out there without me being notified?"

"Fucking media vultures!" she exploded and collapsed against the cushions. But she had a sneaking suspicion Agent Daniels had tipped them off. He must have a reason for wanting to start the media circus, but Chris had no idea what he hoped to gain. It would greatly increase the difficulty of the investigation, as they would now have to navigate reporters calling for interviews and statements, as well as the public calling with an endless supply of mostly useless tips. Shit.

They watched the rest of the story, and Hugh grabbed his laptop to check what the other stations had posted. All the other stations had very similar stories and she fully expected a front-page story in Monday's *Albuquerque Journal.* While he scrolled through the various web pages, she called Finn to make sure he was aware and forewarned of what they would face in the morning. Hugh finally clicked the computer closed and set it aside. She stood and tugged him up from the couch.

"This sucks, Hugh." She reached up to kiss him. "But let's not let it ruin tonight, okay? Starting tomorrow I'm going to be swamped with this shit-show of a case, but for tonight I'm still all yours if you want me."

He wrapped his arms around her waist and lowered his lips to hers. His deep kiss left them both panting slightly. "Definitely. Come to bed."

Chapter Nine

Hugh

He was late to work. He would have been on time, but the gorgeous blonde woman in his bed was simply too tempting. He grinned as he balanced the cardboard tray of coffee cups and reached for the door handle, remembering how he had woken earlier that morning with Chrissy sprawled across his chest, her long bangs hiding her eyes. He'd gently brushed them aside, trying not to wake her, but wanting to see her beautiful face. She had an adorable sprinkle of light freckles across her nose and cheeks he could only see when he was close. He was extremely fond of them. He liked the ones on her shoulders too. He was supremely satisfied with the way the weekend had turned out, especially considering the crappy start on Friday. Chrissy was everything he'd ever dreamed about in a woman: smart, beautiful, sweet-yet-sassy, and amazing in bed. She didn't hold back any part of herself, her physical strength freeing him to meet their needs in ways he'd never felt comfortable exploring before. He and Chrissy simply fit well together in so many ways. He knew he was falling fast and couldn't seem to make himself care.

He slipped in the front door of DeLuca Construction and shut it softly behind him, hoping Izzy was busy in her office. No such luck; she was leaning over Malva's work station and glanced up with an evil smirk as he struggled not to drop the coffee.

"Well, well, well. Look who finally decided to grace us with his presence. Exhausting weekend, big brother?"

"Not at all." He set the tray on the countertop and handed his secretary a cup. "Caramel macchiato for you." He handed one to Izzy. "And a skinny vanilla soy latte for my nosy sister."

"Yes! Plain coffee was just not cutting it this morning. Thanks, Hugh." She took her coffee and reached up to kiss his cheek. "I'm just teasing. There's a fairly decent chance I won't call Chris to tell her to take it easy on you and let you get more sleep."

"That's really big of you, Izzy. Thanks. Sorry I'm late, by the way."

"It's not a problem." She waved his concern away. "Hey, any chance you'd be up for having Janey for a sleepover this weekend? She's been missing her Uncle Hugh and asked about it again this morning."

He realized he'd been ignoring his niece a bit since he and Chrissy started dating and felt horrible about it. He usually had her to stay overnight at least once a month, but he'd been so wrapped up in his love life he'd forgotten about the little girl. "Of course. God, I'm sorry I haven't spent much time with her lately."

"Hey," Izzy said as she placed her hand on his arm. "Don't worry about it. It's fine. She just misses you."

"I miss her too. I love having her over. Let's do Saturday night, okay?"

"I know you love having her and you always spoil her rotten. Maybe I'll see if I can tempt Chris and Cara out for a girls' night. It's been way too long."

"Sounds good. See if Mel can go too; Finn can come to my place and help me with uncle duty."

"Janey will be in heaven. I'll see if the newlyweds can stand to be apart for an evening. All right. I've wasted enough time. I need to get started on payroll." She raised her cup in salute to both Hugh and Malva, then disappeared into her office.

Hugh got his messages from Malva and took his own coffee—a plain, dark brew since he despised the overly sweet drinks his sister and secretary loved—and began returning calls. The first was to the developer of the construction site where the bodies had been discovered, who had left five increasingly frantic messages starting at eleven o'clock the evening before. He must have seen the news. Hugh spent a solid half hour trying to calm him down and assure him they would be able to restart the construction later in the week.

"Hugh, I have too much tied up in this project to let it just sit out there on the West Mesa, blowing all to hell!"

"Yeah, Marty, I know, but there's nothing I can do until the police release the scene. We'll be out there the second they do, okay?" Hugh felt for the man, but he had better things to do than spend his morning placating a nervous developer. He was finally able to calm him down and get off the phone, only to have Malva buzz him on the intercom almost immediately.

"Hugh, there's a Theodore Marcone here to see you. He doesn't have an appointment. Do you have time to see him today?"

Well, shit. The stars seemed to be aligned against him getting any work done today. He sighed and pinched the bridge of his nose. "Yeah, Malva. Send him back." His secretary knew good and well who he was, but she'd never seemed to like him. He stood and crossed the office to open the door. "Uncle Teddy, it's good to see you." He accepted his uncle's hand and pumped it vigorously.

"You too, Hugh. It's been too long." The other man was in his 60s, slim, and rather dapper in a navy suit and purple tie. "Since your brother's wedding, in fact. You haven't brought that beautiful young lady you danced with all night in to the restaurant yet."

His uncle owned an upscale Italian restaurant in downtown Albuquerque. "You've obviously been talking to my parents. I'll be sure to bring Chrissy by for dinner soon. So, what can I do for you? Have you finally decided to open a satellite location in Rio Rancho?"

Uncle Teddy laughed and sat in the chair Hugh

gestured to. "Maybe next year. I'm not quite ready to take the plunge yet. No thanks." He waved away the coffee Hugh offered.

Hugh sat on the sofa across from his uncle with another sigh, resigned to wait until Teddy was ready to talk about whatever had brought him to DeLuca Construction. While Hugh and his brothers and sisters had always called him "Uncle," Teddy was a close family friend and not actually a blood relation. He and Hugh's father had grown up next door to each other in the International District of Albuquerque, where many immigrant families lived. They had both been drawn to the business opportunities that abounded as the population grew in the 1970s, but while Teddy had been attracted by the restaurant industry, Tony had found the booming construction field more to his liking. He'd begun as a day laborer in his father's construction company and learned the business from the ground up, finally taking over when his dad retired. Teddy had been equally successful; Hugh couldn't begin to count the number of times his family had celebrated special occasions at Bella Marcone. He definitely needed to take Chrissy there soon.

"I'm sure you're wondering why I stopped by."

Hugh raised his eyebrows and chuckled. "It crossed my mind. You haven't come to the office since Dad retired."

"True, true. I don't know how he does it. I'd go crazy if I didn't go to the restaurant every day. I'm nowhere near ready to retire." Teddy shook his head as he crossed his legs.

"Well, Mom keeps him pretty busy around the

house and planning for their next trip. So, what can I do for you, Uncle Teddy?" He didn't like to rush, but his do-to list was beckoning.

"Hugh, I owe your father more than I can ever begin to repay. You know he saved my life when we were young, right?" Hugh knew he referred to an incident in their youth when Tony had rescued a drunken Teddy from drowning in a swimming pool. At Hugh's nod, he continued. "He also loaned me a large amount of money a few years ago when the restaurant was going through a hard time. The bank wouldn't consider it, but your dad didn't even hesitate."

Hugh hadn't known about it, but wasn't terribly surprised; his father was generous to a fault.

"Because I care so much about your family, I came to give you some advice, Hugh." He paused and leaned forward to look the younger man in the eye. "You need to make this business at the construction site go away."

Hugh couldn't hide his surprise. What in the world? "I'm sorry, Uncle Teddy, but I have no idea what you're talking about."

"Listen, Hugh. I have business associates who don't want this case to be investigated too deeply. Some things should be left alone." He leaned back in his chair and steepled his fingers under his chin.

Business associates? It seemed Uncle Teddy had some rather unsavory acquaintances. Hugh connected the dots quickly. Well, holy shit. His dad's best friend was apparently involved with the local mob. He had a momentary thought that perhaps his own father also had similar connections but dismissed it almost immediately. His dad was the least likely person to let himself become involved with the mafia. It was ridiculous. Of course it was. But once the thought had occurred, it burrowed its way into Hugh's subconscious in an insidious way. He shoved it away, at least for now, and concentrated on what Teddy was saying. "Why would you think I have any say in this? Bodies were discovered on my job site and the police are investigating. That's all I know." He tried his best to keep his face blank.

Teddy smiled grimly and sighed. "I know your girlfriend and your brother are investigating the bodies. I'm not the only one who knows, either. And now the FBI is involved." He stood and walked to the office door. "Hugh, these are not the kind of people you want to get involved with, trust me."

"What am I supposed to do, Uncle Teddy? I build houses for a living. Finn is the one who carries a gun."

"I don't know, Hugh, but if you care about that pretty lieutenant and your brother, you'd better think of something."

Once his uncle left, he found he was unable to concentrate fully on the tasks he'd set for himself. He finally gave up, shutting his laptop with more force than strictly necessary, and headed out to make the rounds of his active job sites. Maybe he'd make time to stop by for a visit with his father.

***

Chrissy

"Heads up. Agent Dumbass at ten o'clock," Finn said as he returned from the restroom.

Chris choked on her coffee, spilling some on her white blouse as she spun around in her chair. "Goddammit," she muttered, and reached into her top desk drawer for a Tide-to-Go stick. "Just what I didn't need today." It had been brutal dragging herself out of Hugh's bed that morning; she wasn't ready to give up the closeness and isolation they'd enjoyed all weekend in exchange for the headaches of the real world. She also hadn't gotten nearly as much sleep as usual, gladly eschewing extra shut-eye for Hugh's addictive love-making. She was now paying the price with scratchy, dry eyes and a general lethargy. She would dearly love a nap.

"Good morning, Lieutenants." Agent Jared Daniels approached their desks, looking more than ever like a male model rather than a federal agent.

Chris finished dabbing the detergent ineffectually on her blouse, then dropped the tube in her drawer and slammed it. "Well, well, well. If it isn't our newest television celebrity. What are my chances of getting an autograph?"

"Are you jealous, Lieutenant Hart? I'm willing to share the spotlight with you, of course. The camera will love the two of us together." He grinned and winked at her.

Chris wanted to shove her fist into his bright white teeth. "No thanks. I prefer to work behind the scenes. I'm a bit curious why I saw it on the evening news before I heard that we were going public with it."

The FBI agent pulled a chair close to their desks and straddled it. "My superiors and I decided it was better to release it to the media on our terms rather than try to keep it quiet."

"This is your idea of working together?" Finn asked.

"I never said we were working together. I said you were cooperating with the FBI."

Chris entertained a brief fantasy that involved dumping the contents of her coffee mug over his perfect blond waves. The cocky bastard seriously needed to be brought down a few pegs and she'd love to be the one to do it. At that moment, however, she caught sight of Captain Silva coming toward them, so she shoved her desires down for the moment and addressed the FBI agent. "We will certainly do everything we possibly can to assist you, Agent Daniels." She raised her eyebrows at Finn and tilted her head, hoping he'd pick up on her signal.

He caught on without having to turn around. "Yeah. Be sure to let us know what we can do to help."

"Good to see you all cooperating." Captain Silva clapped Finn on the shoulder as he joined their group. "It bugs the hell outta me when law enforcement doesn't help each other out. We're all on the same mission. It shouldn't matter who gets the credit."

Says the man who's already made captain, Chris thought. Out loud she said, "Absolutely. We were just telling Special Agent Daniels how much we appreciated the news story last night." She refused to let Finn's eye rolling distract her. "And he was about to tell us what the FBI has discovered about the other five bodies. He was saying that with the vast resources the FBI has at their disposal, they were able to run the tests so much faster than the state police with our limited lab. I forget, Special Agent, was it the ballistics or the DNA report you brought?"

Daniels stood, crossed his arms, and rocked back on his heels, a small smile hovering about his mouth. "It was the DNA report. I can hardly wait to share it with you."

"Excellent! I'll let you three get on with your investigation. Good to see you again, Special Agent Daniels." Captain Silva shook the FBI agent's hand, then retreated to his office.

"Well played, Lieutenant Hart," Daniels murmured.

Chris was about to respond when she caught sight of Hugh entering the precinct. Her stomach flipped slightly, the way it always did when she saw him after being apart for a while. The receptionist waved him back and he smiled as he saw her. All her self-talk about taking it slow and not letting her emotions get the best of her withered away when he looked at her like that. She wanted nothing more than to throw her arms around his neck and kiss him deeply. Since that would be about the most unprofessional thing she could do, she settled for greeting him with a smile of her own and a soft "hello."

Finn made the introductions, simply calling

Hugh his brother and not bringing attention to the fact that she and Hugh were a couple. Good. It wasn't any of Daniels' damn business.

"I stopped by to see if you and Chrissy were available for lunch. I was in the area and thought I'd try my luck." Hugh winked at her as he spoke.

Daniels inserted himself into the conversation before she had the chance to speak. "Well, Lieutenant Hart and I were going to discuss the DNA report over lunch, but we can reschedule. I'll have the report sent over later this week."

Chris ground her teeth and narrowed her eyes at the FBI agent. *Bastard.* She knew he'd love to take the opportunity to delay, possibly forever, getting the DNA report to her. "No, no. That's all right. Sorry, Hugh, but I already have lunch plans."

Hugh shifted his eyes back and forth between Chris and Daniels. "No problem. I'll take a raincheck, Chrissy."

"I'll see you at home tonight, okay?" She purposely overstated their living arrangements for Daniels' benefit, hoping Hugh would play along. She'd decided she wanted the FBI agent to know she was taken, and was therefore immune to his charm.

He stared intently at her for a long moment. "Sure, no problem, hon." He turned to his brother. "You free, Finn?"

"Sure." Finn looked like he was trying not to laugh. "I'll be eager to read the report this afternoon, Chris. I'll meet you outside, Hugh."

"I'll walk you out." Chris grabbed Hugh's hand as she spoke. "Excuse me for a moment, Agent

Daniels."

Hugh said nothing until they reached his truck. "So, that's the guy from the news last night, huh?" He gestured to the precinct building behind them.

She sighed and dropped his hand. "Yeah. That giant pain in my ass is Special Agent Jared Daniels from the FBI. He doesn't play nice."

"Clearly." He reached for her hand again and tugged her around the side of his truck not facing the building. "Is he here about the bodies found on my site?"

She nodded. "I can't tell you much about it, of course, but yeah, that's why he's here."

He pulled her into his arms and brushed her hair behind her ear. "Chrissy, is there any way you could hand this case off to some other detectives?"

She looked into his ice blue eyes and frowned. "What are you talking about?"

He shrugged, but wouldn't quite meet her eyes. "I was just thinking maybe you and Finn are too close to it, because of, well, you know."

He was clearly a terrible liar, something that would no doubt come in handy in the future. "Hey." She reached up to cup his face in her hand. "What's going on?"

He appeared to be thinking deeply, but said nothing. Instead, he angled his head toward hers and took her mouth. Long moments later he raised his head, leaning his forehead against hers. "Nothing. I'm just worried about you and Finn."

She smiled slightly and brushed her thumb across his full lips. "We'll be fine. This is what we do and we're pretty damn good at it, you know."

He took her fingers in his hand, kissing them as chuckled softly. "I know. Be careful, okay?"

She sensed he wasn't being entirely truthful yet, but decided to let it go for the moment. "Always. Sorry about what I said in there." She jerked her head back toward the building.

"What are you talking about?"

"When I said I'd see you at home later. I wanted to send a message to Daniels, that I'm taken, but I didn't mean to—"

He stopped her words by kissing her again. "Shh," he said against her lips. "What you said was perfect."

She watched him drive away, wondering what he was keeping from her.

"So, he's your boyfriend, huh?" Jared Daniels was leaning against the side of a black sedan.

Chris gritted her teeth and turned to face him. "Are you spying on me now, Agent Daniels?"

"Special Agent Daniels. And no, I'm not spying. I came out to see if you were ready to go to lunch— you do still want to see the DNA report, don't you? Anyway, I didn't want to interrupt your cozy little moment with your partner's brother. Is it just me, or does that seem like a conflict of interest?"

"Shut up. Are we going to lunch or not?"

He took her to Marcello's, an upscale steakhouse in Uptown Albuquerque. She schooled her features as she read the menu so as not to reflect her shock at the prices. *Holy shit! Lunch here is like half my grocery bill for a month!* She searched for the cheapest item and had settled on a bowl of over-priced soup when Daniels spoke up.

"Lunch is on me, of course, Chrissy."

"Oh, well in that case, I'll have the lobster. And you can call me Chris or Detective Hart." Chrissy was reserved solely for Hugh.

Jared smirked as he set his menu on the white table cloth. "Have whatever you desire, compliments of the federal government. I'm on an expense account."

"Your per diem must be a hell of lot bigger than mine." When the waiter took their order, she settled for a small steak and refused the glass of wine he offered. "I'm on duty."

"So am I," Jared said as he raised his glass to his lips. "Life is short. Live a little, Detective."

"I live plenty. Are you going to tell me about the DNA report?"

He set his wine glass on the table and smiled crookedly at her. "Tut, tut, Detective. Can't we enjoy our lunch before talking about such mundane things?"

She took a sip of her iced tea. "I live for mundane things. DNA?"

"Right." He reached into his jacket and pulled out an envelope, which he handed to her. "There's not much. One of the bodies was a close match in CODIS, but the sample was degraded, so it's impossible to be sure. The match is a small-time criminal by the name of Dante Fiore. He was arrested for money laundering and a few other petty crimes; he served a term in the state pen about ten years ago."

"How can he match a dead body? One that's been in the ground for, what? Several decades?"

"Thirty years at least. The DNA is obviously not from Dante Fiore, but our records show he had a twin brother. A twin brother who has been missing for thirty-four years."

Chapter Ten

Hugh

"So, what's with that FBI agent?" Hugh took a sip of the iced tea the waitress had just delivered.

"Agent Dickless? I could give you an earful." Finn set his own tea on the table with a sigh.

Hugh choked on his tea as he laughed. "I'm listening."

Finn narrowed his eyes at his brother. "You're not jealous, are you?"

"No." Hugh shook his head. "Of course not. It's just—"

"What? You can trust her, you know."

"Yeah, I know I can trust her. It's him I'm worried about. That shit-eating grin—"

Finn laughed. "I know, right? Kinda makes you want to shove those perfect white teeth straight down his overly tan throat, huh?"

"Oh yeah. Do you think it's a federal offense to punch an FBI agent in the face?"

"Probably, but if you hit him hard enough he

131

wouldn't be able to talk about it. You might get away with it."

Hugh grinned as he pictured what Finn described. It would be supremely satisfying. "I'm not thrilled with the idea of my girlfriend having lunch with someone like him. I bet he'd get a kick out of causing trouble between me and Chrissy."

"I'm sure he would, but Chris isn't stupid, you know. She's had his number from the very beginning. The only reason she went with him is to get that lab report on the DNA evidence. He's been extremely cagey about sharing anything, but expects total transparency from us. Our captain is breathing down our necks to play nice and cooperate with the FBI, but they have no intention of reciprocating. Bastards," Finn muttered as their meals were delivered.

Hugh dug into his enchiladas, wondering how to bring up the thing he really wanted to talk to his brother about. Chrissy hadn't been at all receptive about it and he knew it would be a tough sell to Finn. He waited until they were both finished, making small talk until the meal was over and they were finishing their tea. "So, why don't you see if you can hand this case off to someone else? It sounds like it's going to be a royal pain in the ass." He tried to appear casual, as if he didn't care one way or the other. In reality, he had his fist clenched under the table, willing his brother to agree with him.

Finn's dark eyebrows drew together, a frown marring his handsome face. "Well, sure, but lots of what we do is a pain in the ass. We'll be fine. I'm actually going to enjoy showing up that insufferable fed."

"I would have thought you might want some easier cases, what with you and Mel being newlyweds and all." He shrugged, as if it didn't matter.

Finn crossed his arms and sat back in his chair. "You're a rotten liar. You always have been. What the hell is going on, Hugh?"

Crap. Finn was right: he'd never been able to pull off the lies his brothers and sisters seemed to have no problem telling. "Nothing. Forget it. It was a dumb idea." He grabbed up the check. "I'll get lunch today." He rose swiftly and headed toward the counter to pay the bill, glad he'd suggested they eat at Eloy's, a Mexican restaurant where patrons paid at the front counter. It served as a convenient disruption to a suddenly awkward conversation. He certainly didn't want to tell Finn about Uncle Teddy's warning and put his father's best friend on the radar of the New Mexico State Police.

Finn joined him at the counter. "Fine. I agree: it was a dumb idea. You care to tell me what brought it on?"

Hugh shoved his wallet in his back pocket and signed the credit card slip. "Nope. Let's just forget it, okay?"

Finn stared at him for a long moment. "Sure. Okay." He reached for a mint in the dish on the counter and tossed one to his brother. "I need to get back to the office."

Hugh mentally castigated himself all the way to his parents' house. All he'd managed to do was make both his girlfriend and his brother suspicious. Yes, he'd seen the patent disbelief in Chrissy's eyes earlier and knew she didn't believe him. He had no desire to lie to either one of them, but he didn't feel comfortable sharing what Uncle Teddy had said. *Shit and double shit.* He absolutely didn't want to be mixed up in this investigation but now he was. His top priority was keeping Finn and Chrissy safe, but if he couldn't convince them to hand the case off to someone else he had no clue how he'd achieve that goal. He was praying he could get some sort of useful information from his father; it was a place to start, at least.

He found his mother in the kitchen, as usual, chopping vegetables for a salad. "Hey, Mom." He dropped a kiss on the top of her head.

"Hugh! This is a treat! I hope you'll stay for lunch." She wiped her hands on a towel and hugged him.

"I just finished having lunch with Finn. Sorry. Is Dad around?"

She released him but stared up into his face, her brow furrowing in concern. "What's wrong?"

Not much got by his mother—it never had. He forced a smile as he pulled away and reached into the refrigerator for a can of soda. "Nothing. I just have a few work-related questions for him."

"Mmm hmm." She glared at him. "He's in the den watching *The Price is Right.*" She turned back to her chopping.

In the den, the television was blaring and contestants were jumping up and down as they were chosen. Hugh flopped onto the sofa next to his

134

dad's favorite recliner. "Hey, Dad. Do you have a few minutes?"

His father clicked the television off and turned to look at his oldest son. "Of course. What's up?"

Hugh took a sip of his soda and tried to think. Now that he was here, he wasn't sure how to broach the subject. "Well, Uncle Teddy came by this morning."

"Please tell me he doesn't need another loan."

"No, no. Not as far as I know." He blew out a breath. "He came to warn me about the case Finn and Chrissy are working on. You know, the bodies found on the Bonatti job site?"

"Why would Teddy know anything about that? The news said it was a serial killer."

Not exactly, but Chrissy had said it was obviously what the FBI agent was hoping the general public would think. Hugh knew better than to share too much information with his father, however. He was sure Finn and Chrissy would prefer he not mention anything about the FBI agent. He decided to go for the bare minimum. "It was a mob hit, actually."

"Ah, shit."

Hugh set his soda on the side table and leaned forward. "That's not exactly the reaction I expected, Dad. Care to explain?"

His father scrubbed his hands over his face. "Your Uncle Teddy is kind of an idiot in some ways, Hugh. He's always been one for shortcuts and get-rich-quick schemes. It's gotten him into trouble more than once, in fact."

"You gave him a loan a few years ago, didn't

you? Why?"

"He's as close as family. I knew he owed money to some rather unsavory people and I didn't want to see him get hurt." Tony stared at his son as if imploring him to understand why he would help his life-long friend.

Hugh sighed. He understood—of course he did—but it didn't alleviate any of his worry over Teddy's visit earlier that day. "And these unsavory people were connected with organized crime, weren't they?"

His father nodded silently.

"Dad, I need more information." How could he make his father understand the urgency of this situation? If he didn't get anything more from this conversation, he was at a loss. He felt the panic begin to roil deep in his gut, churning the enchiladas he'd eaten earlier. He'd have to stop by the drugstore on the way back to work for some antacids. "Please. I'm worried about Finn and Chrissy. I tried to convince them to hand this case off to someone else, but they both refused outright."

"That sounds like your brother." Tony chuckled softly. "And your new girlfriend strikes me as the stubborn sort too. I don't know what I can tell you, son. I don't know anything."

Hugh heaved to his feet and began pacing. "My brother and the woman I—" He stopped, appalled at what he'd been about to say. *The woman I love.* He'd been refusing to let himself even think those words yet, but apparently his heart disagreed with his head. He swallowed audibly and continued. "Finn and Chrissy may be in danger. I need some fucking information, Dad!"

Big Tony stood and crossed the room to his son. "Okay, son. I'll talk to Teddy and see what I can find out. Calm down. Finn and Chris both know how to take care of themselves. They're good cops. Have you told them about Teddy?"

Hugh shook his head, running his hands through his hair. "I don't want to get him in trouble, but if it comes down to a choice between him and them—"

"Let's make sure that doesn't happen. I'll talk to Teddy. I'll go see him this afternoon."

"Yeah, okay." His stomach calmed slightly. "Will you let me know what he says?"

"Of course. I'll stop by the office after I see Teddy." Tony returned to his recliner, clicking the television on again. "We'll make sure they're safe, Hugh. I promise."

***

Chris

She was eager to get back to the precinct and discuss the DNA results with Finn, but Jared seemed inclined to linger over lunch. Since she didn't want to piss him off, she remained until the bitter end, watching him sip a cup of coffee as he slowly ate a piece of cheesecake. She knew he was doing it to annoy her, so she held her seething temper deep inside and refused to glance at her watch. She was dying to smack the stupid little smirk off his beautiful face, but kept her hands clenched tightly in her lap, determined to wait him out. He was absolutely toying with her, no doubt punishing her for forcing his hand about the DNA report, which she was sure he'd had no intention of sharing with the State Police. She wondered why he was so reticent to cooperate; she'd worked with the FBI before and had found the agents to be professional, yet helpful with all facets of the investigation. Special Agent Daniels was something of a conundrum.

"Are you sure I can't interest you in some dessert, Lieutenant Hart? And are you sure I can't call you Chrissy? It gives a whole new aspect to your personality."

"No dessert, and Hugh is the only one who gets to call me Chrissy. I'd prefer to keep this professional, Special Agent."

"Are you always this prickly, Chris?" He raised his eyebrows, daring her to object to his use of her first name.

"I'm only prickly when I'm thwarted, *Jared*." She emphasized his name, smiling coldly across the table. "Why are you being so stingy with information on this case? Are you worried my partner and I will make you look bad?"

He took another leisurely sip of his coffee, then set the cup on the table. "I'm not losing any sleep over it. How long have you and Lieutenant DeLuca's brother been sleeping together?"

She willed herself not to react. "My personal life is none of your business. Let's talk about the case. What else have you discovered that you're not sharing?"

"I just think we'd work better if we get to know

138

each other. I find you fascinating, Chris."

She didn't believe him for a second. He was clearly attempting to distract her from focusing on the investigation, but she had no intention of playing his game. "Have you found anything else about the FBI agent found with the other bodies?"

"Not much. We know Agent Barilla was undercover in the Argyros crime syndicate and had worked his way into the inner circle, but then he went missing. That's about it."

"Argyros? That name has cropped up in connection with some drug busts. It's Greek, right?"

"Yes. They came to power in the early 1970s in New York and Chicago, and worked their way west by the early 80s. They run the heroin trade in this part of the country these days. We would very much like to bring them down."

"I saw way too many kids OD on heroin when I was in uniform. It's a scourge on this city." Chris grimaced as she remembered some of the horrible deaths she'd witnessed over the years.

"It's in El Paso too. Bringing down the Argyros family would go a long way toward slowing down the river of heroin coming into the southwest, at least until another group takes over."

"It sounds like we both want the same thing, Jared. So why are you being so difficult?"

The waiter interrupted them at that moment to deliver the check. Chris had a hard time holding back her frustration as Jared took advantage of the distraction to avoid answering her question. He slipped off to the restroom while he waited for his credit card to be run, then didn't give her a chance to redirect when he returned, insisting he had to hurry back to El Paso. She chuckled ruefully, shaking her head as she watched him practically race out of the restaurant to his car.

Finn was at his desk when she returned to the precinct. "So, did you find out anything from Agent Dickweasel? Did he actually have a DNA report?"

She swallowed her chuckle—best not to encourage his inappropriate humor—and handed him the manila envelope. "We've got a name: Dante Fiore. He's a small-time criminal, but he had a twin brother who hasn't shown up on our radar since the early 1980s. It's a pretty good chance the twin ended up on the wrong side of an angry mobster's gun."

"Well, it's a start, I guess." Finn sighed as he spread the report across his desk. "But it doesn't tell us much about who shot him."

"Hold your horses; there's more." She sat at her desk, leaning back with a superior expression on her face. "I have another name: Argyros."

"And?"

"Our dead FBI agent was undercover in the Argyros crime family."

"No shit? Any chance this stellar family is still hanging around Albuquerque?"

"Oh yeah." Chris leaned forward and logged in to her computer. "According to Ja—Agent Daniels, they're still very much a presence in the southwest, primarily involved in keeping the heroin trade up and running." She figured it was too much to hope her partner didn't catch her near slip-up over Daniels' name.

Finn narrowed his eyes at her. "You call him Jared now? Come on, Chris!"

"Calm down! It's simply easier than 'Special Agent Daniels' all the time. Besides, you get more flies with honey than vinegar."

Finn rolled his eyes and sighed audibly. "Whatever," he muttered and buried himself in research for the next few hours.

Chris knew from experience he wasn't one to stay mad for long, but decided to leave him to his work for a while after finding out which of the two families he was looking into. She was knee deep in the Fiore family—what little she could discover—when her cell phone buzzed in her pocket.

Hugh: Hey beautiful. If ur not totally sick of me yet, can I talk u into a dinner date tonight?

She smiled.

Chris: Definitely. Your place?

Hugh: Nope. I'll pick u up. Wear something nice.

Chris: So, my good jeans, right?

Hugh: Not so much. How about that dress you wore at the wedding?

She smiled crookedly.

Chris: I'll see what I can do.

Hugh: Pick u up at 6.

She glanced at her watch and grimaced. She'd have to hurry if she was going to have time to take a shower and put a little makeup on. "I'm out of here, Finn. I'll see you tomorrow."

"Oh." He glanced up, startled. "You never leave early." He was frowning at her.

"Well, I happen to have a date with your big brother in a little over an hour. Apparently, he's taking me somewhere nice and I need some time to primp."

"Okay, who are you and what have you done with my partner?" He laughed as he said it, so she knew she was forgiven.

"Shut up." She chuckled half-heartedly, but didn't actually find what he'd said funny in the least. How long had it been since she'd paid much attention to how she looked? Finn's words stung a bit and she decided to make sure her boyfriend knew she could bring it when the occasion called for it. The only time he'd ever seen her dressed up was at Finn's wedding, and she knew she could do better. She had a dress hanging in her closet she'd bought on a crazy whim last year and tonight seemed like as good a time as any to debut it. She hoped she had the guts to go through with it.

Once home, she shaved her long legs carefully— tonight was not the time for any unsightly nicks— then jumped in the shower, using her favorite, yet expensive, shower gel. After she dried off, she slathered her body with the matching body lotion and spritzed with the body spray. She donned the lacy black bra and panty set she'd been saving for a special occasion, then set to work blow drying her short blonde hair, wishing there was something different she could do with it. She settled for a bit more gel than usual and tucking one side behind her ear. She carefully slipped the form-fitting dress over her head and slipped into her heels as the doorbell rang.

"Hi. Come in. I'm almost ready. I just need to find some jewelry." She returned to her bedroom and rifled through her meager collection of earrings. She'd never been much for glitzy costume jewelry, but wished she had something a bit more special than the gold chain and heart pendant her parents had given her last Christmas. At least her stud earrings were real diamonds, small though they might be.

"Wow." Hugh whistled as he reclined on her bed. She hadn't realized he'd followed her into the bedroom. "You look incredible and you smell even better. That dress will fuel my fantasies for at least a month. Red is definitely your color, Chrissy."

She spun for him, something she never would have believed herself capable of doing before the advent of this amazing man in her life. The look of appreciation on his face made her feel pretty and sexy, both feelings she hadn't experienced often since her previous relationship fell apart. Of course, she put more stock in her intelligence and independence than looks, but it was nice to be appreciated simply as a woman once in a while. She giggled—also something she hadn't done in quite a while—and returned to her dresser to pick up the necklace.

Hugh stood and stepped behind her to fasten the clasp. He leaned down to run his lips across the soft skin exposed at her neck, causing her to shiver with pleasure and lean back into his arms.

"Mmm." She reached her hand up to stroke his face, the smoothness of his skin telling her he'd shaved again before their date.

He turned her to face him and lowered his lips within millimeters of her mouth. "Is this okay? I don't want to mess up your makeup or anything."

She'd met his ex-girlfriend, so his question didn't surprise her terribly. She vowed never to let something like a little lipstick stop her from kissing him. "It's way past okay," she murmured against his lips. She sank into his embrace, her arms winding around his neck.

"God, Chrissy," he whispered long moments later, his forehead leaning against hers. "I could kiss you all night."

"I'm not stopping you."

"What are my chances of getting a raincheck until after dinner?"

"Pretty damn good."

He chuckled and kissed her again quickly. "I don't know how I got so lucky to have you in my life. You look beautiful tonight, angel."

"You don't look half-bad yourself." He was wearing a dark gray suit with a crisp, navy shirt, open at the collar. She pressed her lips against the warm triangle of skin between his top buttons. "And I think I'm the lucky one."

He tilted her chin up and looked deeply in her

eyes. "Maybe we're both lucky." He smiled. "I hope you're hungry."

"I could eat. Where are we going?"

"Bella Marcone. Is that okay?"

"Wow. Yeah, it's great. I've never been, but I've heard it's really nice. And hideously expensive." She frowned, not wanting him to feel like he had to spend extravagant sums of money on her.

He smiled again and winked at her. "Don't worry about that, Chrissy. I can afford it. Besides, my uncle owns it, so I get the family discount."

Chapter Eleven

Hugh

"You aren't eating much. Everything okay?"

Hugh quickly took another bite of the delicious penne Arrabbiata in front of him, although he didn't want it. His stomach was still upset, no doubt a result of the stress he was under, and the spicy pasta wasn't helping. But he didn't want to pile any of his worry on Chrissy, especially since much of it concerned her continued involvement in the case his uncle had warned him about earlier that morning. "I'm fine. I was distracted by the beautiful woman across from me."

"I never knew you were such a charmer, Hugh. I'm flattered, of course, but I don't want to be the cause of you eating cold food."

"Did you think I was talking about you? Well, that's awkward. I meant that lady over there." He gestured to an elderly woman at the table next to theirs.

"Ha ha." She rolled her eyes as she sipped her

wine.

He chuckled softly, hoping he'd managed to shift the focus from his worries. He hadn't intended to bring her to his uncle's restaurant tonight—in fact, he'd been planning to remain at home this evening, figuring it was probably a good idea to spend some time apart. They'd been together all weekend and had a great time; she was exceptionally easy to be with. He wanted to spend the evening with her, but he also didn't want her to think he was being obsessive or clingy. He knew he should take it slow, play it cool, or whatever other crap the so-called relationship experts were spouting these days, but he just wanted to be with her. His plans for a solitary night had changed when his dad stopped by the office late in the afternoon with more information from Uncle Teddy. Reading between the lines of what his father had told him about their conversation, Big Tony had read his best friend the riot act about having any connection with threats directed toward any of his children or their significant others. Hugh wouldn't be terribly surprised if a mild level of violence had been involved; Big Tony was normally a mild-mannered man, but he was extraordinarily protective of his children. He reported to Hugh that Teddy was appalled at his own behavior and wanted to apologize personally to Hugh. He urged him to bring his "young lady" to Bella Marcone that evening, free of charge. He assured Tony he was only passing on a message from an acquaintance and was sure it wasn't nearly as serious as he'd made it sound. It was more like a suggestion to leave well enough alone than a full-on threat. Hugh wasn't sure he believed it, but Teddy was his godfather, and had always been there for him. He knew his uncle wanted the best for him and frequently urged Hugh to find a nice girl and settle down. Maybe meeting Chrissy and seeing how amazing she was would convince Teddy to be fully on their side. It was most likely a stupid idea all around, but it was some sort of action. He was desperate to do something—anything—to keep her and Finn safe. His stomach roiled again at the thought of the danger this case was causing and he gave up on his dinner, pushing it away slightly.

"You don't like the pasta, Hugh? I'll bring you something else." Teddy appeared behind their table and reached for Hugh's bowl.

"No, Uncle Teddy. It's great. I'm just not very hungry tonight. Sorry. I'll take it home and eat it tomorrow."

"Hmm. Well, I guess I can do that. If you change your mind and want to order something else, though, you let me know." He squeezed Hugh's shoulder. "Are you going to introduce me to this beautiful young lady?"

"I'm Chris Hart." She stretched her hand across the table. "It's nice to meet you, sir. You have a wonderful restaurant."

Teddy, always the flirt, took her hand between both of his and kissed the back of it. "I'm Theodore Marcone. I saw you at Finn's wedding, but we didn't have a chance to be introduced, much to my regret. So, you're my godson's new girlfriend?" He smiled and didn't release her hand.

"Yes, I am." Chrissy smiled, her eyebrows raised in a challenge as she reclaimed her hand.

Teddy laughed and clapped Hugh on the shoulder. "I like her. She seems like she can handle you, Hugh. Now, what can I get you for dessert? The tiramisu is to die for, but we have fresh cannoli too. Why don't I bring you one of each?"

"That sounds great, Theodore. Thanks," she said.

"Call me Teddy, please." He turned and left their table, promising to return soon with coffee and dessert.

Chrissy waited until he was out of earshot. "He's your father's brother, I assume?"

Hugh shook his head. "His best friend. The 'uncle' is honorary."

"I'm sensing some tension between the two of you. What's going on?"

She was entirely too perceptive for his comfort. *That's what I get for dating a detective.* "We had an argument earlier today. This dinner is his way of apologizing."

"What were you fighting about?"

Before he was forced to answer—and he had no idea what he would have said—Teddy returned, leading a waiter who was pushing a cart with coffee service and dessert plates. Hugh caught a frustrated look on Chrissy's face and knew his reprieve would be brief. He forced himself to eat a portion of the two desserts Teddy had presented to them, but couldn't manage more than a few bites. He saw Chrissy's probing glances and narrowed eyes and knew he would have to think of something to tell her. The interminable meal finally ended and Hugh

149

left a large tip for the waiter.

Several hours later they lay tangled in his bedsheets, recovering from an especially vigorous bout of lovemaking. Before they'd left her apartment earlier in the evening, she'd asked if he wanted her to stay the night. He adored her forthright manner and assured her that he did indeed want her to spend the night. She had packed a small overnight bag, saying she preferred not to do the walk of shame the next morning when he drove her back to her apartment. She was curled against his side, her fingers running absently through his dark chest hair. He wished they could remain like this forever and forget the bodies found at his construction site, forget the case she and Finn were working on, forget the danger they were both in.

"Hugh."

It was all she said, but he recognized it for what it was: time to talk. He stilled her hand on his chest, rubbing his thumb across her soft skin. God, he didn't want to screw up what they had, what they were building. "Yeah."

She pushed herself up, crossing her arms on his chest so she could see his face. "Tell me. You've been acting weird all day. What's wrong?"

"It's nothing, really."

She sighed and sat up, pulling the sheet with her. "Hugh, that's not going to work. We've got to be honest with each other if this has any chance of working. If *we* have any chance of working." She reached for his hand. "And I want us to work. What we have is really special to me, but if we can't be honest with each other…" She let the words drift away, unspoken. "Hugh, I think I'm falling in love with you." She bit her lip and stared hard at his chest.

His heart leapt at her admission, but he realized he needed to meet her halfway. He was way more than half in love with her, and he knew he had to be honest if he was going to keep her in his life. And he wanted nothing more than to have her by his side—tonight, tomorrow, and for the rest of his life. The thought should probably terrify him, but instead he felt a sense of peace flow through his entire being, and he knew he could do nothing else than give her complete honesty. He sat up and faced her, taking her hands in his. "Chrissy." He tipped her chin up and kissed her softly. "I'm falling in love with you too. Hell, I've already fallen." He kissed her again, deeply, and wanted nothing more than to make love to her again. But she deserved an honest answer to her question. This was a defining moment in their relationship. "Okay, here goes: Uncle Teddy came to the office this morning. He came to warn me that you and Finn are in danger working this case."

"How in the world could he know that?" She cocked her head, a frown marring her features.

"He claims one of his business associates asked him to pass on the message. Apparently Teddy has been taking out loans from the Fiore family—a well-known local small-time crime organization—for years." His dad had pried the name out of Teddy and passed it on to Hugh.

"Fiore?" she asked innocently.

It was too innocent. "You've come across that

name already, haven't you?"

She nodded reluctantly. "I can't tell you very much, but we have run across that name in our investigation. What was the message Teddy gave you?"

"He said he was told to tell me to tell you to let the investigation go. I was supposed to find a way to convince you to hand it off to someone else. You and Finn are in danger as long as you're working on this case." He stared into her eyes, willing her to understand how worried he was.

She leaned forward and cupped her hands around his face. "Hugh, you need to stop worrying about us. Finn and I are really good at what we do and we're going to find out who killed those men."

"But the danger—"

She kissed him, cutting off his words. "I'm a cop, hon. It's what I do, and yeah, it can be dangerous. But so can crossing the street. I'm always careful; so is Finn."

He kissed her back, then pulled her close, tucking her head beneath his chin. "Chrissy. God, I know you guys are always careful, but I'm freaking out. When I think about you and Finn getting cross-ways with a family of mobsters, my gut starts churning."

"I noticed. You didn't eat more than a few bites for dinner." She sat up and looked directly into his eyes. "Being with a cop can be tough, I know. The divorce rate is astronomical. Maybe you should talk to Mel. She seems to be dealing with being a cop's wife pretty well so far. She might be able to help you."

He stared back, thrilled by her references to marriage, yet still terrified by the thought of the danger ahead for her and Finn. "That might be a good idea. So, there's no way I can convince you to let this case go to someone else?"

She shook her head slowly. "There really isn't anyone else. There are only six detectives in the Albuquerque office and the other four are fully engaged with other cases. Finn and I have fewer cases on our load than any of the rest—mostly due to his accident and then his honeymoon."

Hugh nodded, then closed his eyes and rested his forehead against hers. "I'll talk to Mel. Please be careful."

"Always. I don't suppose there's any way I could talk you into a late-night snack, is there? You must be starving."

He smiled crookedly. "I could probably eat. Let's go raid the refrigerator."

They donned robes against the chill night air and trooped down to the kitchen for a snack. Hugh fixed ham sandwiches while Chrissy poured them each a glass of milk. They sat across from each other at Hugh's kitchen table and devoured their meal. He was still worried, but his appetite had returned as he decided to focus on the beautiful woman sitting across from him instead of the danger she might be in—at least for the moment. "Chrissy, sweetheart, I'm glad you're here." He had so much more he wanted to say to her, but he held back, not sure the time was right.

"Me too." She smiled and stood to take their plates to the sink. "Let's go back to bed."

***

Chrissy

Finn was waiting for her in the parking lot of Dante Fiore's office building at 9:30 the next morning, as she had requested. She rapped on the driver's side window.

"Shit! You scared the crap out of me! Don't sneak up on a guy like that!" He exited the Jeep as he groused.

"It's not my fault you were napping on the job. You not getting enough sleep at night?" She raised an eyebrow and smirked as she asked.

"Being a newlywed is hell on a good night's sleep, you know. But I want to point out that I got here before you. Did my big brother make you late for work?" He smirked right back at her.

"Shut up," she said in an off-hand manner as they entered the building. A quick perusal of the building directory guided them to the fifth floor, where Fiore & Associates was located.

"Good morning. How can I help you?" The receptionist was young and cheerful, seated behind a large podium-type reception desk.

Chris flashed her badge, causing the young woman's eyes to widen. "Is Mr. Fiore available? We'd like to ask him a few questions in connection with a current investigation."

"Let me check," the receptionist mumbled as she picked up the phone. A few seconds later she stood to usher them behind her desk and into the inner sanctum of Fiore & Associates.

The door of an office in the back hallway opened and a middle-aged man wearing a dark suit greeted them, shaking hands and introducing himself. "Detectives, welcome. What can I do for you this morning?" He'd obviously been handsome in his youth, but now showed signs of creeping age and letting himself go, complete with paunch, receding hairline, and fleshy jowls overhanging his bright purple dress shirt.

Chris noted the man looked nervous, eyes darting frequently to the door and a fine sheen of perspiration shining on his high forehead. "We have some questions, Mr. Fiore."

"Okay." It sounded more like a question than an agreement. "I really don't know what I can possibly help you with, but ask away." He ended with a nervous chuckle.

"Mr. Fiore, you had a twin brother, didn't you?" Finn asked.

The man appeared shocked. "Yes, Cosmo, but why—"

"Where is your brother, Mr. Fiore?" Chris took over, the way she and Finn had perfected over months of partnership. They excelled at questioning witnesses, able to feed off each other and keep the person being questioned off-balance.

"I, uh, well, I don't know. He disappeared many years ago."

"A death certificate was filed in 1993," Finn added.

"Yes. Cosmo had been missing for over ten years, so my parents had him declared legally dead. Is there a point to this line of questioning,

Detectives? Besides bringing up unpleasant memories?" Dante appeared annoyed, yet Chris detected an elevated degree of tension in his body.

"We may have discovered your brother's remains, Mr. Fiore." Chris watched him carefully for his reaction.

To her surprise, he simply nodded. "Where?"

"Buried in a shallow grave on the West Mesa," Finn said.

Dante sank wordlessly to the sofa and ran his hands through his thinning hair. "Shit," he muttered. "I saw that on the news the other night. I had no idea it was Cosmo. How do you know it's him?"

"We ran the DNA through CODIS and you showed up. You have a record, Mr. Fiore: money laundering, distribution, and a few assorted misdemeanors."

"Most of those charges were dismissed, Detective DeLuca. Besides, that was a long time ago. A lifetime," he ended on a whisper.

"We knew it wasn't you in that grave and it didn't take long to trace birth records and discover your twin brother, who hasn't been seen since 1982." Chris sat in the chair across from the sofa, winking at Finn.

He got the signal, of course. "Do you have a bathroom, Mr. Fiore?"

"Down the hall." He gestured distractedly toward the outer office.

"Thanks." Finn winked back at Chris and disappeared.

"I'm very sorry for your loss, Mr. Fiore," Chris said when the door had shut behind Finn. "Are your parents still alive?"

Dante nodded. "It crushed them when Cosmo disappeared. Can you tell me what happened?"

"We don't know much yet, but it looks like a homicide. I'm sorry," she added as he groaned softly. He was hiding something, but his grief at the news of his brother's death was real. "Can you tell me anything about what your brother might have been involved in back in 1982?"

"What wasn't he involved in? I loved my brother, but he was always in trouble. He was always involved with the worst kind of people. He was enamored with the criminal lifestyle and figured he was going to be a big shot crime boss someday. Hah!" He laughed harshly and stood to pace in front of his window. "I knew he was dead; he had to be. But I guess I still had a tiny bit of hope that he was out there somewhere, that he'd come waltzing back home one day with a fantastic story of where he's been for the last thirty-four years."

"Do you remember anyone specific he spent significant time with? Any names?"

A shuttered look descended on Fiore's face as he took a seat behind his desk. "I'm afraid not, Detective. That was many years ago. Now if you'll excuse me, I should go tell my parents their son is dead," he said coldly.

"Of course. I am sorry for your loss." She stood and handed him a business card. "Please call if you remember any names."

He took the card, but didn't so much as look at it before he tossed it on his desk.

She nodded curtly and left.

Finn was leaning against the reception podium, flirting with the young woman seated behind it. He straightened as she approached. "Thanks, Missy. You have a nice day."

Chris rolled her eyes as they walked out of the building. "Did you get anything useful from her?"

He shrugged. "She's only been working there for a few months, but she said Dante has a lot of interesting clients. And he leaves the office frequently for long lunches."

"I can't say I'm terribly surprised. I didn't totally buy his grieving brother act, did you?"

"Nope. What's the plan?" He held the door open for her.

"You head back to the precinct and keep digging into the fabulous Fiores. I'm going to stick around and see if Dante goes anywhere."

"Okay. See you back at headquarters, Chris." He ambled toward his Jeep, his limp still noticeable, but much less than it had been even a few weeks before.

She bought a coffee from the food truck parked nearby and then sat behind the wheel of her car, waiting and watching the front of the building she had recently exited. She had only had time to take a few sips of her latte before Dante walked through the front door and hurried to a Lexus parked a few spaces away. She froze, hoping he wouldn't notice her and give the whole thing away. Luck was with her and he entered his car without looking her way. She waited until he had pulled out of the lot, then started her own car and followed him, keeping one or two cars between them.

She had run Dante's home address and parents' address, but he didn't appear to be heading toward either. So much for his story about rushing to console his grieving parents. He led her a few miles away to a large office building, where he parked and disappeared inside. She waited a few moments, then followed, hoping she would be able to figure out who he was visiting. Her luck continued: all visitors were expected to sign in at the front desk. She flashed her badge and perused the visitor log, finding Dante's name with the number 312 written in the box next to it. A quick search of the building directory posted by the elevators revealed Dante was visiting a cyber security firm on the third floor. She took a seat in the corner of the plush waiting room and dialed Finn.

"I need you to run a check on CyberSecure, Inc. Who owns it? Any relatives of Dante?" She disconnected after he assured her he would send a text as soon as he found anything, then settled back to drink her coffee and wait.

Dante reappeared forty-five minutes later, scurrying out toward his car, not noticing Chris. She followed as he finally drove to his parents' house, staying nearly an hour. Finn texted to inform her CyberSecure, Inc. was owned by Benito Fiore, a cousin to Dante.

"From what I could find, Benito is the head of the family. There's nothing rock solid, but it looks like the Fiores do indeed run a small time organized crime syndicate."

"Of course they do. Imagine my surprise," Chris said dryly. "Dante is currently playing the dutiful son, and I shouldn't have had so much coffee this morning."

Finn laughed and wished her luck—or diapers.

She cursed him good-naturedly and settled back to wait, trying not to think about the fullness of her bladder, nor how hungry she was starting to feel. Surveillance was one of her least favorite aspects of the job. It was certainly nothing like Hollywood painted it to be. It was boring in the extreme and often uncomfortable. Dante finally reappeared, and this time led her to a nearby Italian restaurant. She called Finn again to have him check the ownership, but she felt sure it was a family business and Dante was most likely doing double duty: lunch and informing the rest of the fam about Cosmo. Her stomach grumbled loudly and she realized she had most likely discovered all she could with this round of surveillance. The aroma of freshly baked bread from the sub shop two doors down beckoned; she ducked inside to relieve her over-full bladder and grab a quick sandwich.

She juggled her bag containing a turkey sub with chips and bottle of water in one hand while she opened the door and strode back to her car, stopping to stare in dismay at the sight that greeted her: all four tires on her Mustang were flat, obviously slashed while she was inside the sandwich shop. Somebody was sending a message. "Son of a bitch," she muttered and reached for her phone.

Chapter Twelve

Hugh

He followed Bob up the walk to his brother and sister-in-law's house, admiring the fall flowers they'd planted along the brick walkway and the pumpkins grouped on the front porch.

"Hugh! How wonderful! Hello, Bob." Mel answered his knock and stood back to invite them inside. "I just put on some fresh coffee."

Bob trotted in like he owned the place, exchanged butt sniffs with Fluff, was hissed at by CJ, then followed Fluff to the kitchen. Hugh trailed after them and accepted the coffee Mel set in front of him, reaching for the sugar.

"Is everything all right?" she asked.

"Oh, yeah. Of course. I was just in the neighborhood and thought I'd stop by and see how you're doing. I haven't talked to you much since you and Finn got back from the honeymoon."

"Have you seen the pictures?"

He shook his head and quickly found himself

flipping through a slideshow on her iPad, admiring the attractive newlyweds in various poses on the beach, in the rainforest, and at various tourist attractions. Finn had confided to him that Mel thought of herself as extremely average in the looks department, but Hugh completely disagreed. The young woman next to his brother in the photos was stunning, and the love shining from her eyes toward her new husband was unmistakable, as was the utter devotion in Finn's own expression. They looked happy, carefree, and tan—at least Finn did. Mel looked happy, carefree, and slightly less pale than usual. The pictures made him think longingly of being with Chrissy on a sun-drenched beach somewhere, with no danger or dead bodies hanging over their heads. "These are great pictures, Mel. You and Finn look really...perfect together."

She took the iPad back from him and closed the cover. "What's up, Hugh? You seem kind of...I don't know, wistful today. Is everything okay between you and Chris?"

He sighed and stirred his coffee. "She actually sent me to talk to you."

"About?"

"About how you seem to handle being married to a cop so well. You're doing okay so far with the whole 'Finn being in constant danger' thing."

"Oh that." She poured herself a fresh cup and sat opposite him at the table. "Are you and Chris already talking about marriage?"

"No, at least not directly. It's definitely in my long-range plans, though, if I can convince her. But I'm freaking out about the danger she's in, especially with this mob murder case." He didn't want to tell her about Uncle Teddy's warning, so he hedged a bit.

"Well, I'm glad to hear you're serious about her. You guys are great together."

"Thanks. She's amazing. So, how do you handle the stress of being married to a cop? Is it a problem with you and Finn?" He ran his hands through his hair. "I'm afraid it's coming between us."

"You don't want her to quit, do you?" Mel looked appalled.

"No, of course not. But I don't know if I can handle her being in danger all the time."

Mel smiled and reached for his hand. "I know, Hugh. Believe me. I have moments I can't even breathe when I stop and think about what Finn faces every day. But focusing on that and worrying endlessly about it gets me nowhere. It doesn't keep Finn any safer and it just tears at our relationship."

"That's your great advice? Just stop worrying and don't think about it?"

"Kind of sucks, huh? But Finn has almost been killed twice in the last year, and neither episode was in the line of duty. Besides, I love him. He's a cop. I can't expect him to step away from his calling just because I don't like the thought of him facing criminals every day. I guess I could walk away, but that wouldn't make either one of us happy."

He stood to carry his mug to the sink. "Yeah, okay. I guess that's pretty good advice. I sure hope I can follow it."

"You'll find a way if Chris is worth it."

"Well, shit, Mel! Way to just put it out there on

the line!" He leaned against the granite countertop he'd helped install and crossed his arms.

"Sorry."

"Yeah, sure you are. Okay." He pushed away from the counter. "Well, I'm not sure how I'm going to manage it, but Chrissy is totally worth it, so I'll figure something out."

"Good answer." She stood and crossed to the coffee pot, then refilled his cup and set a plate of cookies on the table. "Now sit down and have some of these chocolate chip cookies I made yesterday."

He sat and reached for a cookie. She might be quiet, but she had an air of authority he thought it best not to test. "These are great, Mel. Finn's a lucky guy."

"That's for sure." She ruffled his hair and grabbed a cookie for herself. "It's going to be all right, Hugh. Finn and Chris are careful and they're really good at what they do. We need to believe in them."

"I believe in them. It's all the shitty people they deal with every day I don't believe in."

***

Seamus was the first to arrive later that evening. Hugh had invited his brothers over to watch the 49ers beat the Cardinals, so long as they brought beer.

"The 49ers don't stand a chance, bro!" Seamus pulled a bottle of Rolling Rock from the six-pack he carried and stuffed the remainder in Hugh's fridge. "They switched quarterbacks last week and it was a disaster! You might as well just donate your part of the pool to me now."

"You do know the Cards have three first-stringers out with injuries, right? I like my 49ers for tonight's game." Hugh reopened the refrigerator and selected a bottle of the local craft IPA he'd stocked earlier.

"It's so sad that you continue to back a losing team." Seamus rummaged through Hugh's cabinets for a bowl in which to pour the chips he'd also brought.

Tony and Finn came in together a few minutes later, each carrying a six-pack and a grocery bag. The pizza Hugh had ordered arrived fifteen minutes later and they were soon settled in front of his 60-inch flat screen to watch the game.

"What are the girls doing tonight?" Hugh asked Finn. He knew his sisters and Chrissy were gathering at Finn and Mel's place, but hadn't heard what their plans were.

Finn shrugged. "I think Mel said they were watching chick flicks and drinking wine, but I wouldn't be surprised if they end up watching the game. I overheard Izzy and Cara fighting over which team had the hottest guys." He rolled his eyes as he spoke.

"Was Chrissy there yet?" Hugh asked.

"Not yet. She called to say it was taking longer at the tire shop than she expected."

"Did she get a flat today?" Hugh set his beer down, concerned.

"Four of them." Finn grimaced as he spoke. "Somebody slashed them while she was running surveillance this morning. Put her in a pisser of a mood."

"What?" Hugh set his plate aside and leaned toward his brother. "What happened? Is she okay?"

"Calm down. She's fine, of course. She can handle herself, you know. She was surveilling someone for a case and came out of a sandwich shop to find her tires slashed. No big deal. The department will cover the cost of new tires." Finn stared at his brother like he had two heads.

"Was it in connection with the bodies found on my site?" His stomach tightened in dread as he asked.

"Yeah, but it's just intimidation, Hugh. It's posturing. This kind of stuff happens more often than you might think. "

All the progress he'd made toward accepting what Chrissy did for a living flew out the window, replaced by a bone-deep cold fear, along with a haze of red anger that Chrissy hadn't told him. He bit off a curse and heaved himself off the couch, punching the button on his cell phone to call her as he walked.

"Hey, Hugh. How was your day?" She sounded guarded, as if she knew why he was calling.

"Where are you right now?" He growled the words out.

She sighed audibly. "Dammit, you talked to Finn. I should have told him not to tell you."

"I thought we were going to be honest with each other, Chrissy. This isn't *my* idea of honest." His teeth were clenched so tightly he'd probably have a headache later. He was doing his best not to yell because he didn't want his brothers to overhear.

She was silent for a long moment. "I'm sorry," she finally said. "I didn't want you to worry. My tires were slashed, but we really have no way of knowing who did it. It could easily have been connected with any other case or just be a random thing."

"Oh, come on! That's bullshit and you know it! It was a direct threat by whoever put bullets in those six men we found buried at my job site!"

"No, Hugh, I don't know that! I'm a detective and I deal in hard evidence, not conjecture!" She took a deep breath and continued. "Now, I'm sorry I didn't tell you about the tires. That was shitty of me. But I can't have you freaking out like this about routine stuff that happens while I'm on the job. Finn and I are on this case and there's nothing anyone can do about it. Go watch the game with your brothers. I'll talk to you tomorrow." Then she hung up.

Hugh stared at his cellphone in disbelief. *She hung up on me!* "Nothing anyone can do about it, huh? Well, fuck that." He touched the button to open his contacts and scrolled through until he found the one he was looking for. He pressed the number and waited, tapping his foot impatiently. After five rings, someone finally answered. "Jason? Yeah, it's Hugh. Listen, man. I need a favor."

***

Chrissy

She tossed and turned all night, upset by the fight she and Hugh had had over the phone. She felt bad for hanging up on him, but he seriously needed to calm down about her job. To be honest, it had truly taken her by surprise when he'd freaked out about Teddy's warning. He'd never had a problem—as far as she knew—with her or Finn's job before, so why now? What had changed? She hadn't wanted to tell him about her tires, knowing he would overreact. Keeping secrets was not her style, but she hadn't wanted to deal with his worry. She knew she was falling in love with him, but she was beginning to question the feasibility of a long-term relationship with a man who couldn't accept her career in law enforcement. But she missed him tonight—missed his lovemaking, missed his big body curled around hers, missed him falling asleep while she was still talking, missed him holding her throughout the night—simply missed him. They'd slept together four nights in a row and she wasn't ready to stop, wasn't ready to face the long, lonely nights that had been her life since the end of her last relationship. The plan had been for her to go to his house after the game and girls' night, but then they'd fought, and she'd decided to stay home. And he hadn't called or texted since she'd hung up on him. She checked her phone every few minutes and had even powered it down and turned it on again to make sure it was working. At three a.m. she flung the comforter off impatiently and padded barefoot to her minuscule kitchen. She filled her kettle and set

168

it on the stove to heat while she rummaged through a cabinet for the box of herbal tea she remembered buying a few months ago. She finally found it, then reached into the next cabinet for her bottle of whiskey. She poured a small amount in the mug and sipped while she waited for the water to boil. "Aw, screw it," she muttered and filled the mug, then turned the stove off. She took her mug of whiskey with her to the couch, pulled the quilt her grandmother had given her for high school graduation over her bare legs, and reached for the remote. She brooded and watched inane infomercials for an hour, finally falling into a restless sleep halfway through a tedious ad for Sauna Pants. She woke three hours later with a crick in her neck and a headache from the whiskey. She glanced at her bedside clock on her way to the shower and stubbed her toe on the nightstand when she saw the time. "Shit." She was running late—again. Finn would undoubtedly rub it in.

Forty minutes later, she placed a venti Americano with an extra shot on Finn's desk then slid into her own desk chair and switched on her computer.

"Are you okay?" he asked as he reached for the coffee.

"I'm fine. I want to go talk to Adrian Argyros today." She focused on the computer screen, refusing to look at her partner.

"Because Hugh looked like crap after he called you last night, and you look like crap this morning," he said, ignoring her attempt to keep it professional.

"Thanks, really," she said with a grimace. "Can

169

you hand me the Argyros file?"

"Did you guys break up?"

She shrugged. "I don't want to talk about it." She swung in her chair to face him. "And I would really appreciate if you wouldn't report my every move to your brother."

"Hey, I'm sorry about that, but I had no idea you hadn't told him about your tires getting slashed. He's freaking out about the cop thing, huh?"

She nodded briskly. Every cop was aware of the difficulty in maintaining a healthy relationship with a civilian—they simply didn't handle the stress well. "I sent him to talk to Mel."

Finn nodded. "Good call. She's handling it pretty well. Listen, I'm sure he'll come around. He's crazy about you."

She sniffed and turned back to her screen, determined to not let him see the tears shining in her eyes. She cleared her throat and blinked until her vision cleared. "Can we focus on the case, please?"

"Sure. Let's go talk to Daddy Argyros."

They drove to Adrian Argyros' downtown office, Integrated Solutions, LLC. "What is it with these mobsters and all their nebulous-sounding businesses?" Chris asked as she punched the elevator button for the fifth floor.

"Right?" Finn said with a chuckle. "If they want to keep a low profile, they should go with something less obvious. It's almost as bad as ice cream trucks."

"Or Chinese buffets. Do you think there's anyone who really believes those aren't fronts for something sketchy?"

"And what about all those gold and silver exchange places? Here we go." Finn waved her out of the elevator in front of him.

Integrated Solutions, LLC took up the entire fifth floor and Chris looked around the elegantly appointed waiting room, realizing immediately the Argyros family had to be much more successful than the Fiores. She didn't think Adrian Argyros would be as easily handled as Dante Fiore. The receptionist was male, in his thirties, and looked competent and professional. Chris doubted Finn's charm would have much effect, unless the man happened to be gay. She'd suggest switching their roles, but she sucked at anything resembling flirtation. It was amazing she'd ever managed to get together with Hugh.

"Good morning, Detectives," the receptionist said. "How may I help you?"

They gave each other a side glance at the cool demeanor of the man. They both wore their badges on chains around their necks, but most people still had to ask. "We need to talk to Mr. Argyros," Finn said.

"Do you have an appointment?"

"No, sorry." Finn didn't sound the least bit apologetic.

Have a seat." The receptionist gestured to the plush sofas. "I'll see if Mr. Argyros can fit you in."

He kept them cooling their heels for nearly half an hour. The receptionist finally stood and led them to an office in the far corner of the enormous suite, ushering them inside. The man who rose to greet them was tall and imposing, with white hair and finely chiseled features. The smile he flashed them showcased straight, white teeth, but didn't quite reach his dark eyes.

"Detectives, welcome. I'm Adrian Argyros. Please, have a seat. Would you like coffee? Water?" He came around his large desk and joined them in a spacious seating area.

"Nothing, thanks," Chris said as she sat next to Finn on the dark blue velvet sofa.

Argyros waved the receptionist away. "Sorry to have kept you waiting. How can I help you this morning?"

"Mr. Argyros, your family's name has come up in a recent investigation." Finn jumped right in.

"Would you care to explain?" Argyros' voice sounded tightly controlled.

"Six bodies were found a few weeks ago at a construction site on the West Mesa. All the men were shot, execution style, in 1982. One of the victims was an FBI agent who was undercover in your family's crime organization."

"My family's what? I have no idea what you are referring to." He sat back and crossed his legs, daring them to disagree.

Chris leaned forward, bracing her arms on her thighs. "Listen, Mr. Argyros. We are with the state police, not the FBI. We're not interested in getting involved in their investigation. We just want to identify the other bodies and let their families find some closure."

Argyros narrowed his eyes and frowned. "I'm afraid you have wasted your morning, Detectives. My family has nothing to do with organized crime and I know nothing about the unfortunate incident on the West Mesa."

"What exactly do you do here, Mr. Argyros? What is Integrated Solutions, LLC?" Finn asked.

"We are an advisory group." At their blank looks, he continued. "Financial advice, investment strategies, that sort of thing. It's all perfectly legal."

I'm sure it is, at least on the surface. "Well, thank you for your time, Mr. Argyros. We can see ourselves out." Chris rose and led Finn out of the office.

He waited until they were seated in her Mustang. "So…that went well."

"It went well enough. I didn't expect him to actually admit anything."

"You were just trying to fluster him."

She concentrated on navigating the one-way streets for a moment, then spoke. "That's right."

"Okay. It'll be interesting to see what comes of it." He glanced across the front seat at her. "You missed our exit."

"I'm not heading back to the precinct yet. I want to talk with Argyros' son, Alexandar. I don't know where he works, but I have a home address."

"Ah, I see." He said nothing else until she pulled to the curb in front of a small mansion in the High Desert subdivision in the foothills of the Sandia mountains. The homes in the neighborhood all cost a minimum of a million and a half dollars, at the very least. They walked up a cut stone path toward a set of towering double front doors and rang a bell, which echoed throughout the house.

"Yes?" a disembodied female voice sounded

from a speaker located under the doorbell.

"Ma'am, we're with the New Mexico State Police. We'd like to speak with Alexandar Argyros," Chris said.

"He's not home."

"Is Mrs. Argyros home?" Finn added.

The speaker was silent for a moment. "I'd like to see your identification. Hold it up to the camera, please."

Finn and Chris removed the badges from around their necks and held them up, one at a time, to the lens angled at them from the top corner of the porch. A moment later, the door opened and a slight, blonde woman stood aside to allow them to enter.

"I'm Ariana Argyros. Alexandar is my husband." She was pretty, but looked tired. Chris guessed her age to be around thirty. She welcomed them into the living room, but didn't offer them any other sort of hospitality. She was clearly anxious to get rid of them as soon as possible.

Finn led off with the questions, using his disarming good looks and charm to attempt to set her at ease and get her talking. She didn't respond, seeming too nervous to appreciate his efforts. They got very little information from her, save for a work address for her husband.

"Your husband is an attorney, Mrs. Argyros?" Chris asked.

"That's right." She nodded as she rubbed her hand absently across her stomach. "He's hoping to make partner this year. Please don't ask me any more questions, Detective Hart. I don't know anything."

More like she's scared to death to say anything about what she knows, which I'll bet is plenty. "Of course. We need to be going, anyway." She flashed Finn a pointed glance. They both stood and turned to leave. "Oh, I forgot to ask about your children, Mrs. Argyros! How many do you have?"

Ariana Argyros looked stricken. "None. We don't have any children."

"I'm sorry. I just assumed with a house this big…well, anyway. Have a nice day."

Finn waited until they were in the car to ask. "Care to share with the class?"

She shrugged, a small smile hovering around her mouth. "Just a hunch. It's probably nothing."

They had barely entered the precinct when the booming voice of Captain Silva reached them. "Hart! DeLuca! Get your asses in here!"

They glanced at each other and picked up the pace to their superior's office. "Great," Finn muttered. "What now?"

"Shut the door!" Captain Silva didn't look up as they entered. "Would you two geniuses care to tell me why I've got the governor's office suddenly breathing down my neck about this murder investigation?"

Finn and Chris stared at each other. "I assume you're talking about the construction site murders, sir?" Chris asked.

"Of course! I received a call from the governor's chief of staff asking me to back off from this investigation and let the FBI handle it." The captain sounded calmer now, but his face was alarmingly red.

"Why would the governor interfere? And why would she want us to back off?" Finn asked.

"No idea. The chief of staff, a guy named Keller, wouldn't say."

"Oh, shit," Finn whispered, too soft for the captain to hear.

"I told him, politely of course, to mind his own goddamn business. We clearly have jurisdiction here and are cooperating with the FBI, who, by the way, have shown very little interest in solving anything but the murder of their own agent." He stood and poured himself a cup of coffee from the pot behind his desk. "Now will you two, for the love of God, please get this case solved? I do not need the governor riding my ass about this!"

"Yes, sir. We are making headway." Chris looked at Finn and jerked her head toward the door. "We have reports to write, so…"

"Yeah." Captain Silva gestured for them to leave. "Just get it done, okay?"

"Yes, sir," they said in tandem.

She waited until they were back at their desks. "Spill."

"Listen, Chris. I don't know for sure, but Hugh's college roommate was named Jason Keller, and I remember something about him being big into politics. I think I remember Hugh talking about him getting a job with the governor's office." He stopped and looked at his partner. "It probably doesn't have anything to do with it."

She tamped her anger down and hissed, "It was Hugh." She stood and pushed her chair in carefully.

"I have an errand to run. I'll see you later this afternoon."

Chapter Thirteen

Hugh

"Hey, Malva, could you call the city about those permits—"

The outer office door slammed open, interrupting Hugh and causing Malva to drop her pen.

"I need to talk to you." Chrissy didn't yell, but her eyes were narrowed dangerously in his direction.

Ah, crap. This can't be good. "Why don't we go into my office?" He held the door open for her, ignoring Malva's wide, questioning eyes.

Chrissy said nothing as she preceded him into his office, but he swore he could feel waves of anger rolling off her. Bob dragged himself out of his bed and padded across the office, tail wagging madly, to greet one of his favorite people. Chrissy bent down to pet him and Hugh had a brief hope she might have calmed down slightly.

She gave the dog a final pat and sent him back to his bed before rounding on Hugh. "I can't believe you called the goddamn governor!"

So, that's a 'no' on the calm. She's completely pissed. "I didn't call the governor. I called an old friend of mine who happens to work for the governor." How in the world had she found out so fast?

"Really, Hugh? You're going to split hairs with me now? I don't recommend it."

"Chrissy, hon, I—"

"Don't! I'm not in the mood to hear any of your endearments right now, Hugh! I just got done getting my ass royally chewed by my captain because of you! I can't believe you'd do that to me! Why?" The betrayal on her face cut straight through his heart.

"I'm scared shitless, Chrissy! That's why! You've got fucking mobsters threatening you and slashing your tires! I had to do something! I feel so powerless! I can't stand the thought of anything happening to you or Finn." He grabbed her upper arms and tried to keep himself from shaking some sense into her.

"It's not your job, Hugh! You can't just waltz in and interfere with our job. God! Who the hell do you think you are?" She shrugged his hands away and crossed her arms, breathing heavily, tears shining in her eyes.

He hated that he'd done this to her, hated that he'd made her cry, but why couldn't she understand his desperate need to protect her and his brother? "Can we sit down and talk about this? Please?"

She was shaking her head even before he finished speaking. "I can't. No. I'm not ready to talk about this with you." She swiped angrily at the tears leaking from her eyes and sniffed. "Stop interfering. Period."

"I don't know if I can do that. How can I sit by when I know you're in danger?"

"Ugh! I can't do this, Hugh! I can't be with a man who doesn't believe in me!'

"That's not—I do believe in you!"

"Yeah, well, you have a hell of a way of showing it." She walked to the door and stopped with her hand on the knob. "I'm sorry, Hugh. I think it's best if we don't see each other anymore."

"Are you breaking up with me?" *God, please, no!* He felt like he might throw up right there on his office carpet. He wanted to put his fist through a wall.

She nodded, refusing to look back at him. "It's for the best. Take care of yourself, Hugh." Then she was gone.

He stared at the wood grain of the office door for several long moments before he realized he needed to sit or he was going to pass out. He stumbled to his sofa. *She just walked out on me. Oh, God, she broke up with me.*

"Hugh?" Izzy's soft voice called through the door. "Are you okay?" She peeked around the door.

He didn't look at her, choosing to keep his head resting on the back of the couch, eyes closed. "Not really, Iz."

She closed the door quietly and came to sit next to him, taking his hand.

"You heard, huh?"

"Oh, yeah. Her dulcet tones penetrated into my

office…and possibly the building next door."

He groaned in response. "She broke it off."

Bob whined and left his bed to hop onto the couch next to Hugh.

"Yeah, I heard." Izzy left him for a moment, then returned with a steaming cup of coffee. "Here. Sit up and drink this."

He didn't want it, but he took a sip anyway. "She broke up with me."

"Yes, she did. Why? What did you do?"

He gave her a scathing look over the rim of his mug. "I thought you heard everything? And why do you assume I did something?"

"I couldn't hear everything. And I assume it was you because I know you. I repeat: what did you do?"

He gave up. "I called Jason Keller at the governor's office and tried to have the murder case she and Finn are working on taken away from them."

"Shit, Hugh! You're lucky all she did is break up with you. She does carry a gun, you know."

"Thanks, Izzy. Really. You're a big help."

"You don't need sympathy right now, big brother. What you need is a kick in the ass. What the hell were you thinking?"

He vaulted to his feet, slopping hot coffee over his hand. "Dammit," he muttered and set the mug on his desk. "I don't know! I was trying to protect my little brother and the woman—" He stopped before he said too much.

"The woman you love?" She chuckled slightly at his surprised look. "It's really not a huge secret,

Hugh."

"Shit."

"So what are you going to do about it?" She crossed her arms and leaned back into the couch cushions.

"What do you mean? She said she doesn't want to see me anymore."

Izzy gave him a sardonic look, reserved for times when she was especially unimpressed with one of her brothers. "Seriously? Maybe you don't really love her."

He cursed again under his breath and stared out the window. "I have to get her back."

"I can work with that. She's the best thing that ever happened to you, Hugh, and I've never seen you so happy. When you weren't too busy making yourself miserable about how dangerous her job is, that is."

"The thought of her and Finn in danger makes me physically ill."

"Well, you better figure out what's more important: your stomach or having her. She's a cop, and there's always going to be some element of danger with that. But she was a cop long before you ever met her, so it's not fair to expect her to change her career for you. You need to figure out if you can accept her as she is, if she's worth it."

"She's definitely worth it." He ran his hands through his hair and sighed. "That much I know. What I can't seem to figure out is how to deal with the knowledge she may not come back to me at the end of the day."

"Oh, Hugh." Izzy stepped next to him and put

her arm around his waist, leaning her head against his chest. "There are no guarantees for any of us. I can't promise she won't ever get hurt or worse doing her job. But I can't promise you won't walk out of here and get run over by a bus, either. I think love, the kind of love you and Chris have, is pretty rare. Don't throw it away. Find a way to accept her and her job. Your only other choice is to live without her. Can you accept that?"

He pulled her close and kissed the top of her head. "No. I need her." They were both silent for several moments. He wondered how she had become so wise when he was unaware of any recent long-term romantic attachment in her life. "Thanks, Izzy. Now get out of here so I can figure out how I'm going to get my girlfriend back."

***

It took all afternoon, but he finally came up with something. It was undoubtedly lame, but it was a start. He tiptoed toward her front door just after six p.m., Bob following silently. He quietly commanded the dog to sit directly in front of her doormat, looped the flowers through his collar, then knocked and quickly ducked around the corner.

She opened her door slightly, the chain still in place. "Bob? What are you doing here?" She shut the door, then reopened it after she unhooked the chain. "Hugh?" She stepped into the hallway and looked around.

He stayed hidden, hoping her soft spot for Bob would pave the way for a reunion.

"What's this?" She must have found the flowers and the note.

I'm sorry.

"Hmm. Well, you might as well come in for a while."

He breathed a huge sigh of relief and slipped around the corner—just in time to see Bob's tail disappear into her apartment as she firmly shut the door. He stared stupidly at her front door for several minutes before he chuckled softly and went to sit on the stairs. Twenty minutes later, he was beginning to feel the cold cement under his ass. He pulled out his cell phone and sent her a text.

Hugh: Did you kidnap my dog?

Chris: We're having a drink. He'll be out in a bit.

He shook his head at the thought of his dog enjoying a beer with her while he sat in the hall, clearly not invited. *Well, what did I expect? I guess I'll just sit here and wait until my dog is finished having a drink with my girlfriend.* He refused to think about her as anything else. He would do whatever it took to get her back. Izzy had managed to help him realize what a complete dumb ass he'd been about her job. What had gotten into him? Finn had been a cop for years and it had never truly bothered him before. Hearing about the threats against them had sent him over the edge into some sort of insanity.

She kept him waiting over an hour. He was considering sending another text when he heard her door creak open and Bob padded down the hall, his nails clicking on the concrete.

"Did you have a good time, bud?" At least the flowers were gone and a quick glance at her front door showed she hadn't thrown them on the welcome mat. "This is not exactly how I pictured this going down. I kinda hoped I'd be the one drinking the beer, not you." He could smell it on Bob's breath and shook his head ruefully. "I hope she only let you have a little. All I need is a drunk dog."

***

Chrissy

She stopped by a Walgreen's on the way to work to buy a bottle of eye drops. She sat in the precinct parking lot, leaning against the headrest and waiting/praying for her eyes to clear at least a little bit. *Jeez, I haven't had to do this since college!* Back then it had been due to partying too hard; now it was due to crying her eyes out over Hugh. Breaking up with him had been one of the hardest things she'd ever done, but she knew it was for the best given his attitude about her career. She couldn't afford to fall any deeper in love with him than she already was; her heart simply couldn't take it. Then Bob had shown up on her doorstep last night. She knew Hugh was nearby—of course he was—but she wasn't ready to talk to him. She had wanted, more than anything, to call out to him, to invite him inside. But she knew it would only be a Band-Aid and not a real solution to their problem. It would have been all too easy to allow him to hold her and make love to her, forgetting all about their fight and his negative attitude. So, she only allowed Bob to come inside, enjoying the thought of Hugh's irritation as he waited for her to return his dog. She smiled slightly as she remembered sharing her beer with the Golden Retriever and cuddling with him on the couch. She had briefly thought about throwing the flowers Hugh had attached to Bob's collar in the trash, but couldn't do it. She refused to put them in a vase, though, and rooted around under her sink until she found a crusty old mason jar. She shook her head and checked her reflection in the rearview mirror, relieved to see her eyes had cleared up a bit. She pocketed the eye drops and headed inside.

Finn was already at his desk, tapping away at his keyboard. He glanced up as she sat. "Are you okay?"

She nodded as she turned her own computer on and logged in. "Please don't ask. We broke up. I hope it won't make things awkward between you and me."

"Of course not." He returned his attention to his screen. "I'm sorry, Chris. My brother's an ass."

"Agreed. Let's focus on solving this case, all right?"

They worked silently for nearly an hour. Finn stood to stretch and refill his mug, then sighed harshly when the front door opened. "Agent

Dickbag is here. This day just went down the crapper."

Chris looked up and saw Jared Daniels enter the building, looking extremely pissed. "What now?" she muttered. "Agent Daniels, what can we do for you today?"

He walked briskly to their desks. "You can tell me what the hell you think you're doing." His jaw was tight and she could see a pulse pounding in his temple. "You questioned two members of the Argyros family."

"We did, as part of our murder investigation. Why does that bother you, Jared? We question people every day." She was not in the mood to deal with his uncooperative attitude today.

He leaned down, putting his handsome face within an inch of hers. "Stay out of my investigation. The Argyros family is off limits to you, do you understand? Stick with the Fiore's. They're small time and should be enough to keep the New Mexico State Police busy for quite a while. Stay away from the Argyros family, Detective Hart. I'd hate to see anything negative happen to your career." He finished with a growl and spun on his heel without giving her a chance to reply. He flung the front door open, slamming it against the wall as he left.

"Looks like you managed to piss off the nice FBI agent. Good job, Chris." Finn placed a mug of coffee in front of her.

"Hmm," she murmured as she sipped. "I'd sure like to know why. He's awfully adamant about us staying out of his business. Kind of makes me wonder if there's more to it than not trusting local law enforcement to do it right."

"What are you thinking?" Finn leaned back in his chair with his mug cupped in his hands.

"I'm not sure, but it might be interesting to find a way to look into Special Agent Daniels' financials."

"You think he's on the take?" Finn looked around as he whispered the words.

"I hope not, but it certainly crossed my mind. Shit! I hate this kind of stuff!" She wrenched open her top drawer and rummaged around until she found half a bar of chocolate. She stuffed a large piece in her mouth and sat back, chewing as she tried to regain some sense of equilibrium. She hated the thought of a fellow law enforcement officer betraying his oath to protect and serve.

"So, what are we gonna do about it?"

"Well, we're going to keep investigating the Argyros clan, for starters. Beyond that, I don't know. We need to keep it on the DL until we know more. God, Finn! Why does everything have to be so fucking difficult?"

"Are we still talking about Agent Dickweed?"

"Among other things." She growled the words around another mouthful of chocolate.

"I'll make a few calls. I've got a buddy who might be able to help us follow the money."

"Yeah," she said with a sigh. "I guess we better do that. I'll make a few calls too."

An afternoon of prying into the private life of an FBI agent left her on edge and aching all over. They had discovered nothing unusual about Daniels, except that he spent an inordinate amount of money on video games. If he was on the take, he'd hidden it well. By the time she got home, all she wanted was a long run followed by a hot shower. She threw on a pair of running shorts and a ratty t-shirt, grabbed her keys, and headed out. She made it to her favorite trail in the foothills within fifteen minutes, then settled in for several miles of mind-calming running. Two miles in, Bob finally caught up with her. She'd seen Hugh and his dog a mile and a half earlier, of course—she was a cop, after all, and always hyper aware of her surroundings—but had decided to ignore them.

"Hey, Bob." She took out one of her earbuds to address the dog and stopped to pet him. He wriggled with excitement, then turned and ran back to his master. She stood and crossed her arms. "You followed me?"

Hugh jogged up, looking amazing in his shorts and tight t-shirt, but panting slightly. He wasn't a runner, but had gamely joined her frequently over the last few weeks. "Oh, you know. Bob and I were just out for a little run. It's funny we ran into you, huh?"

Funny. Sure. "Hugh. What are you doing?"

"Fighting for you, Chrissy. I'm sorry. Can we talk?"

She wanted so badly to give in, but she wasn't ready to risk her heart again so soon. It was too painful. "No." She hated the crestfallen expression on his face, but stiffened her resolve. "I'm not ready."

"Chrissy." His voice broke as he whispered her name.

She sniffed and wiped away the tear streaking down her cheek. "I want to finish my run before it gets too dark. I'll, uh, I'll see you. Bye, Bob." She turned resolutely, put her earbud back in, and ran down the path, away from the man she loved.

***

She had just logged on to her computer the next morning when Finn looked past her, grinning.

"Hugh! Hey, man! Did you bring bagels? Best brother ever!" He dug into the paper bag Hugh set on his desk.

"Here, Chrissy." He handed her a paper cup of coffee and a wrapped bagel. It was her favorite, of course: whole wheat sunflower seed with a veggie shmear. Damn it.

She was tempted to ignore his offering, but that would be juvenile. Besides, she hadn't had time for breakfast. "Thanks." She narrowed her eyes at Finn as she sipped the gourmet piñon roast, which was far superior to the swill in the break room. Finn shifted his gaze guiltily and devoted his full attention to the green chile cheese bagel Hugh had brought for him.

Hugh stayed to chat with Finn for a few more minutes, then said he had a meeting and left.

She sipped her coffee silently, staring calmly across her desk at her partner.

"What?" he finally asked.

"Stop butting in."

"I didn't, I swear! He texted and asked if I wanted a bagel. What was I supposed to say?"

She could tell by the way he still wouldn't look at her there was more. "And?"

"And nothing." But it was a weak whimper. "Shit! Fine! He asked about your favorite. What was I supposed to say?" he repeated.

She made a derogatory, dismissive sound and turned her attention to her work.

"Women," Finn muttered and buried himself in his own work. They didn't speak for over an hour.

Her phone buzzed with a text as they were coming back from lunch and a witness interview for a white-collar crime case they were trying to close.

Cara: Girls' night tonight. I'll pick you up at 7.

She sighed.

Chris: Hugh and I broke up.

Cara: I know. He's not invited.

Chris smiled, glad to not lose her friendship with Hugh's sisters. She'd been worried the breakup would cause Izzy, Mel, and Cara to shun her. She should have known better.

Chris: OK. I'll be ready.

Cara: Good. We're going to Anodyne, so wear something fun. No frumpy jeans!

Chris: God! Bossy much?

Cara: Damn straight! See u 2nite.

She put her phone in her back pocket and stared at Finn. "Your wife and sisters don't seem to care I broke up with Hugh. We're going out tonight."

"Makes sense. We're meeting at Hugh's to watch the game." He didn't look up from his computer. "Of course they care about the break up, but they're not about to stop being friends with you."

She thought about Hugh's family while she dressed for the evening. She was fascinated by how close they were, yet they still bickered and nagged each other regularly. They had accepted Mel as one of their own and Chris had secretly hoped they would one day do the same for her. That might be off the table now, but at least she'd still have their friendship.

Cara showed up fifteen minutes early, looking gorgeous in a sheer floral tunic paired with leggings and ankle boots. "Ooh, girl! You look fierce! I decided to come early to make sure you didn't try to rock the post-breakup look."

"Nope. I'm a free agent and see no reason to mope around in sweatpants." She tried to infuse her words with believability. She'd forced herself to put on a dress and heels and had even delved into her seldom-used makeup drawer for a touch of mascara, blush, and lip gloss.

"That's the spirit. We're going to meet Mel and Izzy there, since she had to drop Janey off at my parents' house."

They found a table at the popular downtown bar

and were sipping drinks when Mel and Izzy arrived.

"You look fantastic, Chris!" Izzy said as she hugged her. "What are you drinking?"

"Jack and Coke."

"Sounds perfect. I'm not in the mood for anything fancy tonight."

They flagged down a waiter and ordered appetizers to go with their drinks. Chris was waiting for the awkward conversation; the other women held their peace until the waiter returned with their drinks.

"So…" Mel began. "Are you okay, Chris?"

She looked at the three faces staring back at her and saw nothing but concern in their expressions. She swallowed the lump in her throat and nodded. "I will be. It sucks, but…" she said with a shrug.

"What happened?" Izzy asked.

"Hugh didn't tell you?" She was shocked; she assumed he would have told Izzy, at least.

"I'd like to hear your version."

Although she would prefer not to re-hash it, she realized these women were her friends and had her best interests at heart. "He can't handle my job. He's freaking out about the danger."

"That's Hugh, all right. He's always been overly protective." Cara sipped her margarita for a few seconds. "It annoys the crap out of me most of the time."

"That's pretty much what Hugh told me," Izzy said. "Any chance you'll forgive him and get back together?"

Chris shrugged again. "I can't be with someone who doesn't support my career. I've worked too hard to get where I am to give it up for a guy."

"Absolutely," Cara said while the other two nodded. "Hugh's being an ass about it."

Chris smiled sadly and sipped her drink. "I miss him," she whispered.

"You're in love with him." Mel reached across the table and covered Chris' hand as she spoke.

Chris couldn't speak without crying, so she squeezed Mel's hand and nodded once.

Cara stood abruptly and walked away, returning a few moments later with four small glasses. "I believe this calls for shots."

"Tequila?" Mel asked.

"Of course." Cara raised her glass. "To Chris, a badass cop who doesn't need a man telling her what to do."

The others joined in her toast and slammed back their shots.

Chapter Fourteen

Hugh

He waited impatiently for Izzy to arrive at the office the next morning, pacing in the reception area. She had spent the previous evening with Chrissy and he was desperate to find out what she knew: did Chrissy talk about the break up? Did she tell his sisters and sister-in-law what a complete ass he'd been? Did she mention him at all?

Izzy walked in a few minutes later and stopped short at the sight of her brother stalking back and forth in front of her office door.

"What did she say? Is she ever going to talk to me again? Do I have a chance?"

"God, Hugh, let me at least get a cup of coffee before the interrogation, please?" She pushed past him into her office.

He rolled his eyes, but hurried to fetch her a cup from his own office. Maybe he'd get some answers out of her if he provided the coffee she obviously needed. She looked a bit worse for wear this morning. He returned to her office and placed the steaming mug in front of her.

She grabbed it and sipped, cursing softly when she burned her tongue.

"Rough night?"

She grunted and shrugged. "I was not the designated driver and Janey spent the night at Mom and Dad's house. Let's leave it at that."

He wondered how Chrissy was faring this morning; she could generally hold her liquor pretty well and he'd never seen her tipsy, but he didn't know if she was perhaps trying to get over him. He wasn't proud of himself for hoping that might be the case. He watched his sister sip her coffee carefully for several minutes. "Come on, Iz! I'm dying here. Throw me a bone!"

She shifted her eyes above the rim of the mug and stared at him. "Fine," she said as she set the mug on the desk. "She misses you."

He stared back at her, unbelieving. "That's it? She *misses* me? Ah, hell, Izzy!"

"Yeah, okay." She took another sip of coffee, as if to fortify herself. "Listen, Hugh. You screwed up big time. Chrissy is a career woman. She's never going to be the little stay-at-home wife you want her to be. Maybe she's not—"

"Jesus Christ, Izzy! I never said I wanted her to be a stay-at-home anything! I'm glad she has a career! I just want—"

"What? What do you want?"

"Chrissy!" he exploded and collapsed into a chair in front of her desk. "I want Chrissy. That's all. Sorry for yelling."

Izzy looked like she was trying not to smile. "It's okay. I'll forgive you if you'll fetch me a couple aspirin." She waited while Hugh left her office to get some aspirin from his bathroom. He returned and placed the two white tablets and a small bottle of water in front of her. "Thanks."

"What am I supposed to do?"

"Do you love her?"

"Of course he loves her." Cara leaned against the door frame, a green and white paper cup in her hand. "He's acting like a complete dumbass, but he does love her."

"Do you ever work?" Hugh asked irritably.

"It's fall break for the balloon fiesta, remember?" She sauntered into the office and sat in the other chair.

He had completely forgotten about the International Balloon Fiesta, held every year in October. He had planned to take Janey this year, but it had completely slipped his mind. *God, I've got to get my shit together!* "Is there any way I could convince you two to give me some actual advice rather than double-teaming me about what an idiot I've been?"

"Aww, where's the fun in that?" Cara asked. "But I did actually come here to problem solve. The question is: what are you willing to do to get her back? Beyond plying her with flowers and bagels, that is."

"And beyond sending your dog to do your dirty work," Izzy added.

"I delivered the bagels myself, you know."

"Whatever. She's pissed way beyond flowers

and food."

"Hugh, this is more than a simple misunderstanding," Cara added. "Your crappy attitude toward her job is a deal-breaker."

"I know." He buried his head in his hands. "I'm fine with her being a cop, you know. At least I was until some asshole started threatening her and Finn."

"It totally sucks, and I get you being scared shitless, but calling the governor's office to try and get them removed from the case was way out of line," Izzy said, while Cara nodded in agreement.

"Yeah, okay. I get that. But what do I do? I can't lose her."

"You've already lost her," Cara whispered.

"No." He shook his head and stood to pace again. "I refuse to accept that."

"Calm down." Cara stepped in front of him, taking his face between her hands. "She broke up with you and she meant it. But with some hard work you might be able to get her back."

"Hard work? I'll do whatever it takes."

"Good." She returned to where she had set her over-sized handbag and fished inside. She crossed to him again and handed him the small white business card. "This is the counselor that helped me deal with all the fallout from my divorce. Go see her."

"I don't need—"

"Yes, you do." Both women spoke at the same time.

"Hugh." Izzy took his hand and pulled him back to sit next to her on the sofa. "You are the best big brother in the entire world, and you've always protected us. You've always been the strong one, but if you want Chris in your life, you're going to have to learn to let her be strong too. I don't think you'll be able to do that all by yourself. There's nothing wrong with asking for help once in a while. Go see the counselor."

He stared at the small white card with simple black lettering. "Fine. I'll give her a call. But you two can't tell anyone—not Finn or Mel or especially Chrissy."

"Of course not," Cara said.

"Not a word," said Izzy.

He grunted something unintelligible and returned to his own office, shutting the door firmly behind him. He stared at the card again. Janet Davis, PhD, LPCC, LMHC. *That's a whole lot of letters. Well, buck up and give the woman a call. Chrissy is worth it.* Fifteen minutes later he had his first counseling appointment the next day. *All right. At least it's something. Now maybe I can get my head straightened out so I can accept Chrissy's job and all the danger that goes with it.* He was proud of her, but the thought of the threats Uncle Teddy had passed on were still there, niggling in the back of his mind. He thought he might be able to deal with a general, abstract level of danger in her career, but a direct threat leveled against his girlfriend and his brother was another matter entirely. He simply couldn't let that go. But what could he do that wouldn't further damage the possibility of getting back together with Chrissy? It would have to be something she wouldn't find out about. *Think,*

Hugh! You used to be a fairly smart guy. You earned an MBA before your twenty-fifth birthday. Surely you can—

He sat up straight as inspiration struck. *That's it! I'm a businessman, after all! I should have thought of this from the beginning!* He made a quick check of his bank account balance, grabbed his checkbook from his desk, and left, telling Malva not to expect him back until after lunch at the earliest.

Uncle Teddy was in his office when Hugh arrived at Bella Marcone. "Hugh, good to see you. What can I do for you, my boy?"

Hugh closed the office door behind him and sat in the chair across from his godfather before answering. "I need your help, Uncle Teddy."

"Of course. I'll do whatever I can." Teddy gave Hugh a serious look and clasped his hands in front of him on the desk.

"Good. I need you to tell me how much you owe and who you owe it to."

Teddy sat back, a frown now marring his features. "Hugh, I—"

"No, Ted." Hugh had no intention of being denied. He had come for specific information and he was damned well going to get it. "Do not fuck with me today. How much and who?"

Teddy swallowed hard and named a sum that made Hugh's eyes widen. "Angelo Fiore. That's who holds the note. I can't begin to pay him back right now. The restaurant is just now starting to get back in the black since the recession."

Hugh was writing the check—from his personal account—as Teddy finished speaking. "Here." He ripped it out of the checkbook and handed it across the desk. "Now tell me everything you know about Angelo Fiore."

Uncle Teddy took the check, his eyes bugging as he took in the number of zeros. "Hugh, I can't accept another loan from DeLuca Construction. Your dad already—"

"It's not from my dad or the company. It's my money and it's not a loan. It's a gift, but it comes with strings. I need you to tell me about the Fiore family."

"What are you planning to do?" Teddy opened a drawer and slipped the check inside.

Hugh leaned back in his chair, more relaxed now that he knew Teddy would cooperate. He was in his element, in the world of business where money and information traded hands, rather than Chrissy's world of guns and violence. How could she and Finn stand it? He'd probably never fully understand. "It depends on what you tell me. Now what do you know?"

Teddy sighed and began to talk. "I don't know much about the family personally. I was desperate for money and I knew I could get a quick loan from Angelo. I'd borrowed from him before and paid it back, so I knew he'd come through this time. But apparently Angelo has made some bad investments recently and decided to call in his debts to cover expenses."

"What kind of investments?"

"I don't know. I've heard rumors, but nothing definite. You know the property on the corner of Central and 4th?"

"The old Hotel Amador? That place is a wreck!"

"Yeah, but apparently Angelo thought he could turn it into a popular boutique hotel. From what I hear, he's lost a shit ton of money on it and can't make payroll."

Hugh stood, causing Teddy to do the same. "Okay. I think I can figure something out from what you've told me. I expect a phone call if you hear anything else."

"No problem. I appreciate this, Hugh. I really do. I wish I knew some way to show you how much it means to me."

"You're family, Teddy. DeLucas take care of their family." As far as he was concerned, that was the end of it. He gave his godfather a hug and left, grabbing a quick sandwich to take back to the office with him. He had a long afternoon of research ahead, but he was hopeful for the first time in weeks.

***

Chrissy

She rounded the corner into the park, near the end of her five-mile run, and saw Hugh sitting on a bench, a large cooler at his side and Bob at his feet. Her heart leapt stupidly while she told herself she was annoyed and fixed a frown on her face. She bent down to pet Bob as he trotted to her, wriggling in delight.

"Hey, Bob." She rubbed his silky golden ears and kissed him between his eyes. "Hugh, what are you doing?"

"I think it's pretty obvious. I'm not giving up." He gestured to the cooler. "I brought dinner."

"Oh, Hugh." What was she going to do with him? He looked completely adorable, sitting on the park bench with a hopeful expression on his handsome face.

"Come on, Chrissy. You've gotta eat. It's a beautiful evening for a picnic. I brought some wine."

Oh, he didn't play fair. She was out of wine at home and hadn't relished the thought of running to the grocery store. It had been a frustrating day and she'd made very little progress on the murder investigation, and none on the one into Jared Daniels. She hardened her heart and prepared to turn him down and finish her run. "Fine. I guess one glass would be okay." Where did *that* come from? God, how pathetic could she get?

He grinned and turned to open the cooler. He pulled out a bottle of chilled Sauvignon Blanc and poured her a plastic cupful. "Here. Have a seat while I get the rest."

She sat and stroked Bob's head while Hugh spread a plaid tablecloth on the grass beside the bench. He unpacked fruit, a loaf of French bread, and several varieties of cheese. It was perfect and romantic. She wished she wasn't a sweaty mess, but decided it was his problem. He gestured for her to sit across from him and proceeded to prepare a plate of food, which he handed to her. "Thanks for staying."

"Thanks for asking." She took a sip of the wine,

cool and crisp, just the way she liked it. "You're not very good at this whole break-up thing, you know?"

"That's for sure. I kinda suck at it, huh?" He sipped from his own plastic cup and winked at her.

She stared at him for a moment, then felt laughter bubble up. "Yeah, you do." She turned her attention to her plate of food for a few minutes, enjoying the creamy Brie and sweet grapes. "This is great, Hugh. Thanks."

"Of course. How was your day?"

She shook her head; she couldn't figure him out. They'd broken up, yet here they were, enjoying a romantic picnic supper in the park as if they were still dating. How was she supposed to move on when he did this sort of thing? "Fairly frustrating, actually. I've hit a brick wall with the case."

"I'm sorry, Chrissy. I know you'll figure it out, though." He topped off her wine as he spoke.

It was nice sitting across from him, enjoying a simple meal without any of the stress that had marred their relationship right before the breakup. "Did you play football in high school?"

He looked taken aback. "Where did that come from?"

She shrugged and reached for more cheese and bread. "I'm enjoying this. I don't want to ruin it by fighting. I want to talk about anything other than my job."

"Fair enough. Yeah, I played football, but I was better at baseball. I played all four years and got a scholarship."

"Did you ever want to go pro?" She realized they hadn't had time to talk about things like this before and was eager to find out as much as she could about his past. She pushed away the pesky thought that it wasn't strictly her business any longer.

He smiled, a bit self-consciously it seemed. "Sure, but I wasn't nearly good enough. What about you? I can't picture you as a cheerleader."

She laughed and sipped her wine. "Hardly. I ran cross country and played tennis."

"Do you still play?"

"I still have a racket, but it's been years."

"Well, maybe you could teach me." He smiled at her, then looked down at his plate.

She frowned slightly at this rare hint of vulnerability from him; he was usually so strong and confident. "Maybe." She cleared her suddenly clogged throat and changed the subject. It was such a pleasant evening and she was loath to ruin it with anything related to their relationship. She had no idea where it was heading, but she knew she wanted to be with him, if he could only find a way to calm down about her job. But for the first time in days she was hopeful.

He produced chocolate chip cookies for dessert that tasted homemade, with big chunks of dark chocolate and crisp pecans in a buttery cookie.

"These are amazing. I'm going to have to run an extra couple of miles to work them off. Did you make them?"

"Uh, no. I stopped by Mel's place this afternoon and she was baking. I mooched enough from her for the picnic." He took a bite of his own cookie. "Oh, wow. Jeez, these are good. I'm glad Finn had the good sense to marry that woman."

Chris laughed and reached to wipe a bit of chocolate from the corner of his mouth, stopping suddenly when she realized she no longer had the right. "Sorry," she whispered and awkwardly pulled her hand back. "You have a little chocolate…" She gestured to his mouth.

He wiped it away, sucking the chocolate from his thumb and flashing her a crooked smile.

She bit her lip, concentrating on not launching herself across the blanket to kiss him like she wanted. Instead, she ate the last bit of her cookie and brushed the crumbs from her fingers before standing to leave. "Thanks for the picnic, Hugh. It was really nice. I gotta go. I'll, uh, I'll see you." She turned firmly and put her earbuds in so she wouldn't be tempted if he called out to her.

The next morning, she had a hard time focusing on her work; the picnic kept intruding upon her thoughts and she found herself re-examining and analyzing every word he'd said and every look he'd given her. She knew he was trying to win her back—he hadn't exactly tried to keep it a secret—and she knew she was softening. But she had to stay strong; unless and until he could learn to accept her career choice and not go behind her back, trying to sabotage her, he was off limits. How, exactly, she would know when or if he attained this magical acceptance, she had no idea. With that rather depressing thought, she turned her full attention to her casework.

Finn was busy filing a report on another case they'd closed the day before, which left her free to continue her investigation of FBI Special Agent

Jared Daniels and the Argyros family. Neither was going particularly well at the moment, however. What little she could find on Daniels showed him to be squeaky clean, and she was at a brick wall with the Argyros family. She worked fruitlessly until lunch.

"I'm starving," she said to Finn as she stretched her back. "You ready to grab a bite? I'm kind of feeling like Italian today."

"Can't. Sorry. I have physical therapy." He stood and grabbed his jacket. "I shouldn't be too late getting back." He was down to every other week for PT and hoping to be released entirely soon.

"No problem. Want me to bring you something?"

"Nah. I'll grab a sandwich or something on the way back."

She chose a small Italian restaurant Finn had introduced her to. Some family member or connection owned it and they always got the best service. It wasn't nearly as upscale as Bella Marcone, where Hugh had taken her, but it was perfect for a weekday lunch. The waitress had just set a glass of iced tea in front of her when Jared Daniels took the seat across from her, smiled at the waitress, and ordered a tea for himself. She was angry with herself for being surprised; she was slipping if she didn't realize she was being followed. She refused to consider the possibility that he was so skilled she hadn't noticed.

"Make yourself right at home, Jared."

"Well, thanks, Chris. Don't mind if I do. So, what's good here?" He reached across the table to

207

snag her menu.

"The calzone, so long as you're not in too much of a hurry. It takes a while to bake, but it's to die for."

"I have all the time in the world."

When the waitress returned, they both ordered the calzone.

"So, why are you following me? Did you purposely wait until Finn wasn't around?" She tried to appear nonchalant as she sipped her tea.

"Absolutely. He doesn't seem to like me for some strange reason. Besides, I wanted to talk to you alone."

She had a theory as to why they didn't get along: something along the lines of two ridiculously good-looking men not being able to share the same space, but she held her tongue. "Well, here I am. So long as you aren't as pissy as you were the other day, I'm listening."

"Yeah, sorry about that. You caught me in a bad moment." He waited while the waitress delivered their salads. "You've been prying into my background, Detective Hart. Find anything interesting?"

Damn, the FBI must have way better resources than the lowly state police if he already knew about it. "You like *World of Warcraft* and *Madden NFL* way more than you should. I didn't find much beyond your video game addiction." Why try to lie her way out of it? It was best to counter his brash accusation with boldness.

He chuckled as he dug into his salad. "It's how I blow off steam. I hate running." He added the last comment with raised eyebrows and a head tilt toward her. "I'm not on the take, you know. That's, of course, why you and Lieutenant DeLuca decided to pry into my records."

She was inclined to believe him; his words had the ring of truth and they hadn't found anything suspicious. "Then why are you being so difficult about this case? I've worked with the FBI before and never had this much trouble."

"I'm going to tell you, Chris, because you've been such a stubborn pain in my ass, and if I don't, you'll keep poking your beautiful nose into the FBI's business until you find something. But you may just get a good man killed along the way, so I'm going to tell you what you have no business knowing."

She toyed with her salad while she waited for him to continue; she didn't dare speak and inadvertently cause him to change his mind.

"We have someone undercover in the Argyros family and he's close to the top. I need you and Finn to back off. We can't afford anything that might cause Adrian Argyros to start looking at his people too carefully. I'm prepared to give you something fairly juicy in return for you forgetting where you put the Argyros file."

"It would have to be extremely juicy because I have an exceptional memory."

"How does the identity of the murderer of the six bodies found on Mr. DeLuca's construction site sound?"

She barely managed to keep from choking on her tomato. "It sounds fairly juicy. How long have you known about this person?"

"Not long; don't fret, Detective Hart. I can almost read your mind." He sipped his tea as he smirked. "You are calling me the most appalling names in your mind right now, aren't you?"

"You have no idea, Jared," she said through gritted teeth. "Tell me the fucking name."

He had the audacity to chuckle. "Ah, here's our calzones. They look delicious, don't they?" He smiled again at the waitress, nearly causing her to drop Chris's lunch in her lap.

She waited until the waitress had walked away, grinding her teeth as Jared made a production out of pouring marinara over his calzone and cutting into it.

"This is wonderful," he said around a mouthful. "All right. You've been patient and I sense you're about to launch yourself across the table and punch my teeth in." He reached into his suit coat and extracted a business-sized envelope. "The name and address of the man is inside." He handed it across the table to her. "He's retired now, but a few decades ago he was the top 'fixer' for several of the crime organizations in the southwest."

She ripped the envelope open and pulled out the single sheet of paper. "George Staphros, aka Georgi the Weasel. Current alias Grady Smithson. And you have evidence he's the shooter?"

"I'll have it sent over this afternoon, as soon as I have your word that you'll drop the Argyros case."

"But wasn't this Staphros hired by them? How do I make a case against him without mentioning the Argyros family?" She folded the sheet and slid it back into the envelope.

"Let the FBI handle that aspect of it. We can make sure it all happens without our guy being exposed. I'll need your word, Chris, otherwise the evidence stays with me."

She would love nothing more than to throw the envelope back in his face, but she and Finn had made zero progress on the case lately and had a mountain of other cases waiting for their attention. "Yes, fine. You have my word we'll leave the Argyros case alone. I still reserve the right to continue the investigation into the Fiore family, however."

"Not a problem. I'll have the evidence file sent over later this afternoon. Now, let's enjoy the rest of this delicious meal in peace, shall we?"

He was as good as his word; the evidence file on George Staphros arrived a little over an hour after she returned to the precinct. Finn had returned a few moments earlier, but looked so exhausted by his physical therapy she decided not to tell him about her impromptu lunch with Jared; he'd most likely be too annoyed to see the benefit of the deal she'd taken on their behalf. It could wait until tomorrow when his pain wasn't directing his mood quite so much.

She was quietly reading through the file—a comprehensive account of the crime and evidence the FBI had compiled against Staphros—when her cell phone buzzed with an unknown number. "This is Chris."

"Detective Hart?" The voice was female and sounded afraid.

"Yes. Who is this?"

"It's Ariana Argyros. I need to speak to you, Detective. Alone. Can we meet, please?"

Chapter Fifteen

Hugh

"Mr. Fiore will see you now."

Hugh stood and followed the receptionist back to the ostentatious, yet slightly shabby office of Angelo Fiore.

"Mr. DeLuca, how do you do?" Angelo stood and came around his desk to shake Hugh's hand. "I'd heard you'd taken the reins at DeLuca Construction. It's a pleasure to meet you in person."

"The pleasure's all mine, Mr. Fiore."

"Angelo, please."

"Of course. Call me Hugh."

They spent a few minutes in polite conversation as Fiore asked about Hugh's parents and other family members before getting down to business. "What can I do for you today, Hugh? I doubt this is purely a social call."

"I'm here to talk about the Amador building, Angelo. Word has it you're looking for investors." Hugh sat back in the chair he'd been offered and waited.

The man across the desk from him looked slightly taken aback. "I don't recall mentioning that to anyone. How in the world would you know about my interests in the Amador Hotel?"

"Well, word gets around in our business, you know. My company would be very interested in investment opportunities related to that property, or an outright sale, if you're so inclined."

Slight frown lines appeared between the man's eyes. "What's your interest in that property? The local media are calling it nothing more than an eyesore."

"Well, it is that, but I can see a lot of potential; lucrative potential to the firm with enough capital to get it going." He watched Fiore carefully for signs of interest.

"And DeLuca Construction qualifies, Hugh?"

"Yes. I've been actively looking for such an opportunity to diversify our interests beyond residential building. The Amador may fit the bill."

"The Amador is a decrepit money pit. I spent too much acquiring it and now do not have the funds available to renovate." He'd apparently decided to be honest. "I would be interested in selling it outright, but I can't afford to let it go cheaply. I'd do better to use it as a tax write-off."

"I'm prepared to pay fair market value."

Fiore sat back, clasping his hands across his rather expansive middle. "What's the catch?"

"Why should there be a catch to fair market value?" Hugh felt the need to push a bit farther before he lowered the boom on the real reason for his visit.

"You show up here, out of the blue, offering fair market value for that run-down shit-hole I was suckered into buying and expect me to believe there's no catch?"

Hugh smiled calmly, then leaned forward to look the man in the eyes. "Fine. Here's the catch: I will pay fair market value plus five percent for that shit-hole and pull your broke ass out of the mess it's currently in. In return, you will cease to threaten my family and my girlfriend in perpetuity. They will be in absolutely no danger from you, your family, or any of your associates—present or future—starting now. And here's a little bonus: if you don't agree to all my terms, I will call the state building inspector and have the property condemned. I promise you I can make that happen."

Angelo Fiore didn't react beyond a slight widening of his eyes. He remained silent for several moments before finally responding. "I wondered about the name. How many DeLucas could there be in a town as small as Albuquerque? Detective DeLuca must be your brother. And you're dating the lovely Detective Hart? How cozy." He stood and laughed harshly. "You're a real son of a bitch, DeLuca. Fine. I need the money more than I need the police off my ass. They won't find anything anyway. I'll have my lawyer draw up the paperwork. We'll be in touch." He extended his hand.

Hugh stood as well and shook the outstretched hand. "I've been called worse, Angelo. I'll wait for your call."

He left the downtown office and drove to his second counseling appointment. The first had gone well and he was hopeful he could get a handle on his fears. Surprisingly, the therapist had spent quite a bit of time having him talk about his failed relationship with Lauren and the resulting depression he'd apparently suffered without realizing it. His counselor, Janet, had pointed it out matter-of-factly and said it was part of the issue he was currently experiencing with Chrissy. But she was positive and upbeat about his ability to learn some coping skills. And he desperately wanted to find a way to authentically cope so he could get her back. One of the hardest things he'd ever done was let her walk away last night after the picnic; he'd ached with the need to touch her. He was initially shocked when she agreed to sit and eat with him because he'd fully expected her to leave him sitting on the park bench with the damn cooler. Mel had been a huge help earlier in the afternoon, not only giving him the freshly baked cookies, but also making a list of everything else he needed for the meal. He never would have come up with French bread and Brie on his own, much less perfectly chilled Sauvignon Blanc. She'd also advised him to be ultra-relaxed and not bring up his dumb-assery. He'd told her she sounded just like Finn, but he hugged her anyway.

The second session with Dr. Davis went well, but it was even more emotionally wrenching than the last, and he ended up needing a few minutes in the bathroom afterward to splash his face and recover. *Damn, digging into all my feelings is rough! But if it helps me get Chrissy back, it's worth it.* Dr. Davis had asked him to recount the story of what had happened to end his relationship with Lauren, and then what had happened with Chrissy. They had spent most of the session talking about similarities between the two and how he reacted. She was helping him realize his over-protective tendencies were causing damage to his relationships and see that keeping Lauren's betrayal a secret was creating a wall between him and his family. *God, I don't relish the thought of telling my parents and siblings about the abortion. Jeez, it's going to crush Mom.*

He was looking forward to a quiet evening with Bob, having decided to give Chrissy a break from his relentless pursuit for a night. Maybe he just needed to regroup and strategize for the next phase of the operation. Last night had gone well, but he was unsure how to capitalize on his success. He was working on his second beer and trying to decide whether he was hungry enough to order a pizza when the doorbell rang. *Aww, crap. I don't want to see any of my brothers or sisters tonight. Please be UPS, please be UPS!* He seriously pondered not answering, but after the second ring he set his beer down with a sigh and strode to the door, fully planning to get rid of whoever it was. He wrenched the door open and froze when he saw Chrissy on his doorstep, hands on her hips, panting from her obvious run.

"Hi. Can I come in?"

"Um, sure. Of course." He stood aside and ushered her inside. He had no idea why she'd

217

voluntarily sought out his company and decided his wisest course was to let her take the lead. But he could at least be hospitable. "You want a beer?"

She smiled crookedly. "I think water might be a better idea for now. Could I get a raincheck on the beer?"

"Of course, yeah." He went to fetch her a bottle from the kitchen. He returned to find her sitting on the edge of an armchair in the living room, perched as if ready to take flight. Bob leaned against her, his head resting on her thigh, while she absently stroked his ears. "Here."

"Thanks." She opened the bottle and took a few gulps. "Sorry to just show up like this. I can go if it's not a good time."

"No, it's fine." God, when had talking to her gotten so awkward? He reached for the remote and clicked off the evening news. Still, he had no idea what to say to her.

She toyed with the top of her water bottle, not looking at him and clearly uncomfortable. "So, how was your day?"

He raised an eyebrow skeptically. She ran all this way for small talk? "Uh, fine. It was okay. Yours?"

"Fine." More fiddling with the lid, which she then dropped on the floor. "Shit," she muttered and began looking around on the floor.

"Chrissy, hon, leave it." The endearment slipped out as he watched her fumble under the sofa. "It doesn't matter."

She set the topless bottle on the table and stood. "I'm sorry. This was a terrible idea. I should go." But she made no move to walk away.

218

He tamped down on the hope that flared at her apparent reluctance to leave and stood, crossing to stand nearer. She smelled amazing; a mix of her shampoo, the perfume that always drove him insane, and perspiration from her run. He knew he was in a bad way when she even smelled good to him when she was sweating. "Hey. What's wrong? You can tell me anything, you know." He was horrified to see her dissolve in tears. It was completely unlike her.

"I'm so-sorry. I shouldn't have come, but I talked to Finn and I made him tell me. He didn't want to, and Mel wouldn't say anything because she promised Izzy, and Izzy promised you, and I don't want you to be mad at any of them—"

"Whoa! Slow down, sweetheart." He dared to step forward and pull the now-sobbing Chrissy into his arms. "Shh. It's okay." He crooned nonsense against her hair as she clung to him. He had no idea what she'd been trying to say, but knew it must be important for her to be this upset.

It took a few minutes, but she finally calmed down enough to pull away and wipe her eyes ineffectually. "Could I have a tissue?"

He slipped away and grabbed a box from the downstairs bathroom, handing it to her as he led her back to sit beside him on the sofa. "Now, why don't you try again. What did you talk to Finn about?"

She sighed, but it sounded more like a hiccough. "He was trying to hint that I needed to talk to you and give you another chance because he knew something. I didn't care for the stupid veiled hints and I made him tell me."

"How did you do that?" He didn't know whether to be amused or horrified at what his brother might have said.

"I threatened to tell Mel that he doesn't take it easy on his leg at work. He spilled everything." She sniffed and reached for another tissue.

Poor Finn. "And what did he tell you?"

She looked straight at him. "He said you're going to counseling. He said it was to help you come to grips with me being a cop." She reached for his hand. "Is that true?"

He should have known his sisters wouldn't be able to keep it secret for long. "Yeah, it is. I told you I'd do whatever it takes to get you back, Chrissy. And I don't have a problem with you being a cop, at least in the abstract. It was the specific threats that freaked me out and made me do the dumbest thing I've ever done in my entire life."

"Oh, Hugh." She stepped closer, dropping his hand as she reached to cup her palm on his cheek. "Is it working? How are you feeling about the danger now?"

He closed his eyes, reveling in the feel of her fingers stroking his skin. "I've only been twice, but it's helping. Dr. Davis is pretty good at getting me to open up." He reached up to cover her hand with his own. "It's a work in progress, but if it means I might have a chance of getting you back someday, it's worth it." He brought her hand to his lips. "Chrissy, please. Please tell me there's still a chance for us." He stared into her beautiful face, loving her so much he thought he might burst, and willing her to change her mind about them.

She stared back, a small frown between her eyes. Then she leaned forward and kissed him softly. "Yes. There's still a very good chance for us." She spoke the words against his lips.

He wondered for a moment if this was real. Maybe he'd fallen asleep in his chair while watching the news and was dreaming that she was here, in his arms, telling him she would give him another chance. If it was, he planned to enjoy it to the fullest. He pulled her tightly against him and took over, kissing her with all the yearning he'd held at bay for the last few weeks. She wasn't pulling away. She slid her arms around his neck and tilted her head, opening her lips under his, welcoming his warm tongue against hers. He kissed her deeply for several moments before pulling back and framing her face in his hands. "Please tell me this is real. It's not a dream or anything, is it?"

She laughed softly and kissed him again quickly. "Of course it's real. If it was a dream, I'd smell better."

He smiled and leaned down to run his lips along her salty neck. "You smell amazing. You taste even better." Then he sat up, suddenly serious. "I swear I'll keep going to my counseling sessions, Chrissy. Please say we're back together. Are we 'us' again?"

She smiled and nodded. "If you still want me."

"If I haven't made that clear by now—"

He was interrupted by Chrissy launching herself at him, pushing him down on the couch as she lay on top and began to kiss him in earnest. He had just enough mental capacity left to pull back slightly and sit up. He stilled her hands against his chest and

221

prayed she would understand. "There's something I need to get out in the open before you hear it from someone else. It's part of the 'work in progress'."

She raised her eyebrows and sat up. "Uh oh. This doesn't sound promising. What did you do and how much is it going to interfere with my investigation?"

"Okay, I deserve that, but I hope what I did doesn't actually interfere at all. I simply approached the problem from a different angle."

"And what angle would that be?" Her voice sounded dangerous now.

"A business angle." He took a deep breath. "I bought the Amador Hotel today."

"O-kay. I'm not sure I understand what this has to do with my case."

"I bought it from Angelo Fiore. Shh." He put his finger against her lips as she tried to speak. "Hear me out, please. Then I swear you can rip me a new one." He waited while she crossed her arms and sat farther away, waiting for him to continue. "I found out from Teddy that Angelo Fiore was upside down with an investment property, the Amador on Central and 4th Street. I went to see Angelo and offered to buy it at fair market value with the caveat that he and his organization stop the threats or anything else that might put my family or my girlfriend in danger. He was desperate to dump the property, so he agreed. That's it. I used my business skills to neutralize the threat against you and Finn. I don't think it interferes with your investigation and it doesn't mean I don't think you and Finn can't handle yourselves or—"

She put her fingers against his mouth to stop

him. "Shh. Yeah, okay. I guess I can deal with it. You just can't help yourself, can you? That protectiveness is deeply ingrained, and I suppose I can learn to live with it so long as you don't try to get me pulled off any more cases. 'Work in progress' indeed." But she smiled as she spoke and leaned in to kiss him.

He kissed her back briefly, then pulled away slightly. "I need to say something else and then I fully plan to make love to you all night, if you'll let me." He rubbed his thumb over her soft lips. "Maybe this isn't the right time, but I need to tell you. I'm in love with you, Chrissy, deeply and completely. And I'm trying to learn how to love you the way you deserve to be loved. I need you to know this before we move on with our relationship." He searched her face, willing her to understand what he was trying to impart.

She smiled radiantly. "Well, that's a very good thing, because I'm completely in love with you as well. I'm not sure I know anything about how to love you like you deserve, either, but I'm going to try. And as for making love to me all night, I'm totally okay with it."

He pulled her back into his arms and down to the couch cushions again and proceeded to do exactly that.

***

Chrissy

She propped her forearms on Hugh's broad chest

and stared at his handsome, sleeping face. God, she'd missed him so much, missed being with him like this. They were still on the couch, having made love twice, and then fallen asleep. Her grumbling stomach had woken her up a few minutes ago, but she was loath to pull away from Hugh's warm, intoxicating body long enough to forage in his kitchen for something to eat.

"What time is it?" he grumbled, eyes still closed.

"No idea." She reached for his left arm and found his watch. "Just after nine. I'm starving."

"Yeah, I can feel your stomach complaining against mine. Let's order a pizza."

"God, yes." She leaned down to kiss him quickly before vaulting off the couch. "Sorry about the puppy breath. Do you mind if I grab a quick shower while you call in the order?"

He sat up and stretched. "Not at all. Your breath is fine, but your toothbrush is still upstairs. Hey." He grabbed her hand before she could run off. "Stay tonight. Please?"

He had that vulnerable look again. She stopped and leaned down to kiss the top of his head. "Of course. I'll need a ride back to my place in the morning." She skipped up the stairs and was soon luxuriating in Hugh's spacious, hot shower. She toweled off and slipped into the fluffy robe Hugh had bought for her, one of many thoughtful little gestures. She stared at her reflection as she ran a comb through her short, blonde hair; she looked happier than she had in weeks, a light shining in her eyes that had been missing since the breakup. *I love him so much and I want to spend the rest of my life with him.* She knew this deeply in her soul and recognized its absence in any of her previous relationships, even Greg, with whom she'd lived for two years. Hugh still had some work to do regarding his fears about the dangers of her job—the purchase of Fiore's hotel was a close call—but she felt sure he was committed to at least trying. She wasn't asking for perfection; she certainly couldn't give it in return. But they were headed in the right direction finally. She frowned slightly as she realized she was still missing some important information that could make or break this newly-repaired relationship.

He was standing at the kitchen counter opening a bottle of wine when she slipped behind him and put her arms around his waist. He had donned a pair of sweatpants, but his muscular chest was still bare. "Hey."

"Hey yourself." He finished extracting the cork, then turned to pull her into his arms. "You smell even more fantastic now." He turned his attention to kissing her neck, slipping her robe off her shoulder and letting his lips follow. "Pizza should be here in a few minutes," he murmured against her skin.

"Hugh, can I ask you something?"

"Anything." He pulled her robe back in place and looped his arms loosely around her waist.

"Well, I know it's way too soon and I don't want to presume or anything…"

"Chrissy." He brushed her damp hair out of her eyes. "Spill."

She shrugged, now unsure she should go so far. "I just…I think we should get some things out in the open." She took a deep breath and plunged in. "I want marriage and kids, Hugh. I'm not expecting it right away or anything, and I'll never be a perfect stay-at-home mom, and I think a woman can have a career and a family, but I need to know it's at least a possibility with us. I assumed it was with Greg, and then it turned out he never wanted that, and it really hurt. I just need to know if…if you want the same thing. Someday." She finished on a whisper and stared at the center of his chest, unable to look into his eyes, afraid of what she might see.

"Chrissy, love." He tipped her chin up, forcing her to look at him. "Of course I want that. And I want it with you. Rest assured I'll be asking sooner rather than later." He kissed her softly. "You know you tend to babble when you're nervous, don't you? It's kind of adorable, especially since you're usually so tough and badass."

She laughed self-consciously. "Only with you. Sorry, but it matters, and I got burned last time."

"Not a problem. I'm just grateful you haven't pulled your gun on me yet. How many?"

"How many what?"

"Kids. I'm curious, since I come from a large family."

"Oh. Well, not six. I don't know how your mother did it and kept her sanity. I was thinking more like two or three."

He chuckled and hugged her. "Two or three sounds perfect."

"Good. Whew. I feel better and I'll stop talking about it now, because your life must be flashing before your eyes." She had to give him props for

226

not freaking out on her. He'd been a bachelor for a long time, and it couldn't be easy to contemplate such a huge life change. She also didn't want him to feel pressured; she'd needed to know there was hope for a future with him, though.

"Not even close, sweetheart. I'm feeling nothing but contentment right now. And hunger. Thank God," he finished as the doorbell rang. He kissed her nose and jogged out of the room, returning moments later with a giant pizza box. "Here we go: half Hawaiian, half pepperoni and green chile. Can you grab the wine and some glasses, hon?"

They ate on the sofa, making a fair dent in the pizza and polishing off the bottle of pinot noir. Then Hugh took her upstairs to bed.

The morning sun was beginning to lighten the bedroom when she pried her eyes open. Golden brown orbs stared back at her from the edge of the bed. "Morning, Bob."

"He's excited you're here. Me too." Hugh scooped her back against his large frame, spooning with her as he kissed her shoulder.

She sighed happily and wriggled against him, enjoying his groan. "I can tell." She rolled over and kissed him. "As much as I would love nothing more than spending the day in bed with you, it's going to have to wait. I have a ton of work. Can you drop me at my apartment?"

"Of course. Why don't you bring some stuff over tonight? I'll clear out a drawer." He said it casually, as if her answer didn't matter. She suspected it mattered quite a bit.

"That sounds great." She kissed him again,

letting her hand stroke across his delightfully furry chest.

"Mmmm. If you keep that up, you're gonna be late for work." He let his own hand slip down to her bottom, where he stroked once, then swatted her playfully. "Get out of my bed, woman!" He threw back the comforter and pushed her toward the edge.

"Tyrant," she mumbled, but dragged herself away from the temptation his body presented. She dressed quickly in her jogging shorts from the night before. "God, I have to do the walk of shame in my running clothes."

He laughed as he stood to pull on a pair of jeans. "I'll put some coffee on."

***

An hour later, she was fully dressed and in her own car, but she didn't drive to the precinct. She'd texted Finn to tell him she had an early appointment and would see him later. She felt bad about the fib, but Ariana had insisted on total secrecy. She drove to the small motel on the outskirts of town, parked, and knocked on the door of room 20B.

Ariana answered the door, opening it a mere crack with the safety chain engaged, then closed it. She reopened and stepped back to allow Chris to enter. "You weren't followed, were you?"

"No. And I did a quick recon of the parking lot. Nobody is watching. You're safe." Chris handed the other woman the cup of coffee she'd brought for her.

Ariana's hand shook as she accepted the cup.

"For now. It won't last. As soon as Alexandar figures out I've left—"

"We'll make sure you're safe, Ariana, I promise. I've arranged for a safe house until the trial. Then you'll go into witness protection."

"Do you really think I'll last that long?" She laughed once, mirthlessly. "Adrian will find a way to have me killed. I know and I accept it. I was the one stupid enough to marry the son of a well-known mobster, after all."

"Why did you marry him then?" Chris had wondered since she'd first met the woman. Ariana wasn't stupid; on the contrary she had a doctorate in microbiology and had been a successful research scientist until her marriage to Alexandar Argyros.

Ariana shrugged and shakily sipped her coffee. "He was charming and swept me off my feet. It didn't hurt that he was rich, either," she added. "I didn't know about his family until we were engaged, and by then it was too late. Alex would never have let me go."

"And now you're pregnant." She'd suspected it the first time they'd met. She'd slipped her personal cell phone number to Ariana before she and Finn had left, hoping she would call at some point. She finally had yesterday afternoon, insisting upon a private meeting in this crappy, out of the way motel. She'd told Chris she couldn't bear to raise her child as a member of her husband's violent, criminal family.

Ariana nodded and angrily wiped away a tear. "I need to stay alive long enough to have this baby. I'll do whatever you want to make that happen."

"I'm going to make sure you stay alive to be a mother to that baby, Ariana. Adrian Argyros does not have the kind of reach you think he does."

"You're incredibly naïve, Detective Hart. But I know what I must do. I've brought all the records I could get my hands on and I'll testify as much as you want. You just need to make sure the trial is after the baby is born. I won't let any of them see me while I'm pregnant. They can never know about this baby. Did you bring the paperwork for me to sign?"

Chris handed her the contract she'd had Lauren draw up yesterday. Contacting Hugh's ex had been a difficult pill to swallow, but she was a professional and knew she needed to work with the D.A.'s office regardless of personal issues. "Do you have a place for the baby? I mean, in case…"

Ariana glanced up sharply. "I'm working on it."

Chris flushed at being caught in her lie. She knew Ariana would likely not live long past the trial; the Argyros family would never suffer such a betrayal and they had enough resources to devote to locating her.

"Here." Ariana handed her the signed contract. "Is it happening today?"

"Yes," Chris said absently as she looked over the paperwork. "I'll take you to the safe house and make sure you're settled. Then we'll make the arrests. I need your cell phone, Ariana, and all your credit cards. I've brought you a burner phone, but I have to emphasize the danger of calling anyone you know that Alexandar also knows."

The woman fished in her over-sized handbag for

her wallet and cell phone. She handed Chris a handful of gold and platinum credit cards and an iPhone. "Fine. I certainly don't want anyone else to suffer. I'm ready."

Chris nodded, admiring the courage of the woman sitting across from her. Would she, herself, have the kind of nerve to do what Ariana was about to do, all for the love of her unborn, unknown child? She thought about the difference between this kind of love and the callous disregard Lauren had shown for her own unborn child. She vowed to do everything in her power to keep Ariana safe, but feared she had very little ability to carry out this vow. "Let's go."

She helped Ariana gather her few belongings and walked her out to her car, checking first to make sure it was safe. They made it to the safe house without incident and she got the other woman settled in with her protective detail. Then and only then did she make the other phone call.

Chapter Sixteen

Hugh

He whistled as he let himself into his office the next morning. He had stopped by for bagels and coffee but was still the first one to arrive. He was setting up a platter in the break room when he heard Izzy arrive. "Hey, sis. In here with bagels."

She paused at the door of the break room, a sheepish expression on her face. "What's the occasion?"

"No occasion. I just got up early and had time to spare." He was going to make her ask, the little tattle tale.

"Oh." She sounded deflated and he had to turn away to hide his smile. "So, nothing happened?"

"Like what? Oh, wait. I forgot to tell you…" He let his words drift away as he pretended to struggle with the lid to the cream cheese.

"What?" She approached eagerly.

"I got tickets for *Lion King* for Janey and me this weekend. You don't mind if I steal her Saturday night, do you?" He bit his lip to keep from laughing at her crestfallen expression.

"That's it? You didn't talk to Chris? She didn't call you?"

"Chrissy? No." He frowned and pretended to think. "She hasn't called me in nearly two weeks." He turned and prepared a bagel for Izzy. "Here. You don't deserve it, you little rat, but I love you anyway. You and Cara just can't keep a secret, can you?"

"So she did call you? Are you back together?"

"She did not call. She came over. And yes, we are back together. Thank God. I was going nuts without her." He took a huge bite out of his own bagel.

"Ohh!" She punched him lightly on the arm. "We tried, but we had to tell Mel! It's not my fault she tells Finn everything! And it worked, didn't it?" She hugged him with one arm while holding her plate with the other. "I'm so happy for both of you!"

"Yeah, me too. I'm going to marry her, by the way. Don't get excited! I haven't popped the question yet, but it's coming soon." He waited patiently while she squealed and jumped up and down. He watched her, so obviously thrilled for him and Chrissy, and wondered—for the millionth time—what had happened to her. He would love nothing more than to discover the identity of the man who gotten her pregnant then left her to raise Janey on her own. Someday he'd find out and he'd rearrange the bastard's face for him. He couldn't even countenance other, darker, reasons for her situation.

"When? Oh, Hugh, this is amazing! I'm so happy for you!"

"Try to contain yourself, Iz. I still need to ask and she still has to say yes. I don't know why I even told you. You'll probably squeal to her before the day is over."

"I won't! I swear!" She took a bite of her bagel and rolled her eyes in delight. "Mmm, why are carbs so delicious?" She set her plate down and boosted herself onto the counter. "I repeat: when?"

"I don't know. I just got her back, and I don't want to rush her into anything. Soon. That's all I'm ready to say. I'm not getting any younger, after all."

"God, Hugh! You're thirty-four, not sixty! And I'm thirty-two, so shut it about being old, okay?"

"Yeah, okay," he said with a short laugh. "I kind of thought I'd have my life settled before I turned thirty, that's all. What about you, Izzy? Do you ever want marriage? More kids?"

A shadow crossed her features, quickly replaced with a smile that didn't quite reach her eyes. "We're not talking about me right now." She slid from the counter and threw her plate in the trash. "Don't worry about me, Hugh. I'm fine. Really. I have Janey and she's everything. I don't have any regrets."

He put his arm around her and pulled her against his side. "Who was he?"

She shook her head even as she hugged him back. "It doesn't matter. Please stop asking me."

"I don't know if I can do that, Izzy. You're my little sister and I hate that I can't fix this for you."

She laughed and poured herself a cup of coffee. "Why am I not surprised? It's my life, big brother, and I'm happy. Let it go."

"Easier said than done." He flinched as she punched him again. "Fine, okay. I'll try. That's all I can promise."

She kissed him on the cheek and escaped to her office.

He blew out a breath and ran his hands through his hair. *God, she's a piece of work!* He went to his own office and put in a few hours of work. Angelo Fiore had sent over the paperwork for the Amador purchase, so he printed it out and went over it with a fine-toothed comb. It was nearly lunchtime before he signed the document online and sent it back to Angelo's lawyer. He stood to stretch his back and decided to swing by the precinct to see if he could sweet talk Chrissy into having lunch with him. He caught sight of a florist as he drove and made a split-second decision to pull in.

"Are those for me? How did you know roses are my favorite?" Finn grinned and propped his feet on the edge of his desk. "It's been ages since you brought me flowers, bro."

"Hilarious. Really. Where's Chrissy?"

"No idea. She's still at her appointment, I guess."

"What appointment? She didn't mention anything this morning." He didn't like the sudden clenching in his gut and tried to ignore it.

Finn shrugged and removed his feet from the desk. "She didn't elaborate. I figured it was lady-stuff and didn't ask. This morning, huh? Does that mean what I think it means?" He wiggled his eyebrows up and down suggestively.

Hugh rolled his eyes. "This isn't middle school, Finn." He reached into his pocket for his cell phone.

Hugh: Hey, where r u? Finn said you had an appointment? Everything OK? Will you be back in time for lunch?

He stared at the screen, but no response came; it didn't even register that she'd read the text. He dialed her number, but it went straight to voice mail. "Goddammit! Where is she?" His stomach was full-on roiling now.

Finn tried to reach her, as well, with the same results. "Shit! This doesn't feel right. I gotta go."

"Where?"

"I'm thinking Angelo Fiore might have finally made good on his threat." Finn looked grim as he checked his gun.

"But I made sure he wouldn't," Hugh sputtered.

"What are you talking about?" Finn demanded.

Hugh told him about the deal he'd made with Angelo Fiore and the purchase of the Amador Hotel. "He swore he wouldn't touch any of my family or, or—"

"Yeah, well, that's what you get for trusting a low-level mobster. I'll call you as soon as I know anything."

"You've gotta be fucking kidding me! I'm coming with you!"

"Hugh, I don't have time...oh, fine. Let's go. But you do exactly as I say! Got it?"

"Hurry up!" Hugh shot the words over his shoulder as he headed out the door.

Finn broke every speed limit on the way downtown. Hugh led the way into the office suite, having just been there a few days before.

"Mr. DeLuca!" Fiore's receptionist sputtered as he slammed the door open. "Mr. DeLuca!"

Hugh sprinted past her and sent the office door crashing against the wall. "Fiore! Where is she?"

Angelo Fiore froze, a sandwich halfway to his mouth. "What are you talking about?"

Hugh rounded the desk and pulled the rotund man up by his tie. "If you have touched one single hair on her head, I will fucking destroy you!"

"Hugh!" Finn grabbed his brother by the shoulders and pulled him away from the older man. "Let go!"

Hugh let go reluctantly, but stuck his face in Fiore's. "Where is Chris Hart?"

"I don't know what the hell you're talking about!"

"Stop, Hugh! I swear to God I'll cuff you if you don't knock it off!" Finn again pulled his brother away from Fiore. "Now get over there!" He pointed to the opposite side of the room. "Shit! Everyone just calm the fuck down!" He continued in a calmer tone. "Now, Mr. Fiore. Do you know where Detective Hart is right now?"

"I have no idea! Why would I know where she is? We made a deal, DeLuca! I didn't touch your goddamn girlfriend!"

Finn stared at the man for several moments before approaching his brother. "I think he's telling the truth, Hugh."

Hugh slid down the wall, his head in his hands. "Where is she?" He knew something bad had happened; she would have answered her phone otherwise.

"I don't know, but Fiore didn't have anything to do with it. Let's go." He turned to address Angelo Fiore. "Sorry for the misunderstanding, Mr. Fiore. We'll see ourselves out."

The man nodded stupidly, his necktie under his right ear.

Finn helped Hugh to his feet and pushed him quickly out of the office. "Goddamn it, Hugh!" He waited until they were in the parking lot to explode at his brother. "You're going to get me in a shit ton of trouble! We'll be lucky if that asshole doesn't file a lawsuit against the State Police! Calm down! Jesus!"

"Sorry." Hugh shook him off and kicked the tire of Finn's car. "Fuck!"

Finn unlocked the door and slid behind the wheel, leaving the door open. He checked his phone for any messages or missed calls.

Hugh threw himself into the passenger seat and followed suit. Nothing. "Now what?"

"I don't know."

They sat, not speaking for nearly twenty minutes. Hugh felt like he might explode if they didn't hear from Chrissy soon. Where in God's name could she be? He was about to suggest they return to the precinct and have an APB put out on her when Finn's phone rang.

"It's her," he told his brother and touched the

screen to answer. "Chris, where are you?"

"Let me talk to her—" Hugh began, reaching for his brother's phone, but was silenced when Finn shoved his palm in front of Hugh's face and glared at him.

"What? How did that—oh, my God! Yeah, I'll meet you there." He slipped his phone into his pocket and started the car. "She's fine. Buckle up. I don't have time to take you back to the precinct, but you will stay in the car, understand?"

"Where is she?" Hugh growled.

"She's with the FBI. I don't have time to explain right now, but she's safe." He accelerated quickly, causing the tires to screech as he pulled out of the parking lot.

***

Chrissy

"You're lucky I was still in Albuquerque, Chris." Jared Daniels slid into the booth across from her, glancing disdainfully around the small, somewhat grubby diner. "Nice place."

She'd chosen the restaurant because of its location—tucked away in the International District of Albuquerque, more commonly known as the War Zone. The city was valiantly attempting to rebrand the area, but long-time residents were a hard sell on the new name. "I didn't choose it for its ambience. I want this little get-together to be as quiet as possible. The coffee's not terrible."

"So, why all the secrecy? What have you got?"

He waved the waitress away as she approached, ignoring the sneer on her face as she shoved her order pad back in her apron pocket.

"Well," Chris said, pausing to sip her coffee from the thick, stained mug, "I have recently acquired some rather damning evidence against Adrian and Alexandar Argyros. Rather a lot of evidence, in fact. I thought you might like to see it."

He grimaced at her. "And I thought we agreed you would stay out of my investigation. What happened to our deal? I acted in good faith and gave you the name of your murderer."

"And I kept my part of the bargain, so calm down. I got a phone call yesterday afternoon from Ariana Argyros. She wanted to meet—alone. She wouldn't talk to anyone besides me."

Jared crossed his arms and leaned back against the cracked vinyl of the booth. "And what did she want?"

"She's willing to turn state's evidence against her husband and father-in-law. She also provided several file folders full of bank statements, both personal and corporate, which I think you'll find very interesting."

"What's the catch? Why the sudden change of heart from Miz Moneybags?"

Chris smiled grimly and sipped her coffee again. "She's pregnant. The catch is she wants out. Full protective custody until after the trial and a witness protection program once hubby and daddy-in-law are in prison."

"She'll never live that long. Once Argyros finds out he's been betrayed by his own daughter-in-law, he'll stop at nothing to have her killed. And a child? No way will he ever let that go."

"She knows all of that. She's lived with them for nearly a decade and she knows exactly what will happen to her." Unbidden, the memory of Ariana's grim, yet brave face rose in Chris' mind. "No one else can know about the baby, Jared. It's crucial to keep it a secret from as many people as possible so word doesn't leak out. She's got some plan in place to make sure the baby is safe. She'll only agree to testify after the birth."

Jared blew out a breath. "Well, shit. This is not exactly how I pictured this going down. Don't get me wrong, it's huge break, but there's a whole lot of moving parts. Where is Ariana now?"

"I've got her at a safe house. We need to move on this soon—today—before Alexandar realizes she's gone. The assistant D.A. is on her way here with arrest and search warrants. I think we should go in with a joint state and federal show of force."

"I need to notify my guy on the inside so he's not taken by surprise." He reached for his cell phone and sent a brief text.

"Are you going to pull him out?"

"Not yet. I'd like to wait and see if this evidence is enough to make charges stick." He was still looking through the files when Lauren arrived.

Chris looked up to see the petite, beautiful woman enter the diner. She saw Chris and hurried toward the table, sliding in next to her. Chris performed the introductions, amused to note the flare of interest in Jared's eyes. She realized she should probably hate the woman for what she'd done to Hugh, but found her emotions more complicated. She was, of course, righteously indignant on his behalf, but she admired Lauren's professionalism and obvious intellect. Selfishly, she was grateful he was no longer involved with the other woman. "Were you able to get the warrants?"

Lauren nodded and handed them to Chris, who read them quickly and handed them across the table to Jared. "The extended protective custody has also been arranged for Mrs. Argyros. When will the arrests be made?"

Chris looked across the table at Jared, eyebrows raised in question.

"This afternoon. We need to move on this quickly. Detective Hart, gather your officers. I'll make a few phone calls." He excused himself and slid out of the booth.

"How's Hugh?" Lauren asked quietly.

"He's good. We're, uh, we're really happy."

"Good. I still care about him, you know. I wish him all the best. I just couldn't be what he wanted." She looked embarrassed at sharing so much. "Well, good luck with your arrests. Give my office a call later and let me know how everything turned out so I can get to work on the case. God, this is going to be a tough one." She stood, shook Chris' hand, and left the diner.

Jared returned to the booth, signaling for the waitress. She directed a scathing look at the back of his head, but sauntered to the table, pad and pen at the ready to take their lunch order. Once they were alone again, he spoke. "My agents will ready within the hour. Yours?"

"Of course. They'll meet us at Argyros' downtown office."

"Where's your partner in all this?"

"I'll call him when we're done here. I told him I was at an appointment all morning, so there's no reason to distract him now." At Jared's amused look, she hastened to explain. "Ariana doesn't exactly trust men right now. I suspected the pregnancy when we questioned her a while ago, so I gave her my personal cell number before we left. I'm the only one she'll talk to at this point. It was her main condition. Finn will understand."

An hour and fifteen minutes later, Chris pulled into the parking lot a block away from the Argyros' building. The three state police units were arriving and she saw Jared standing next to several unmarked, yet obviously Fed vehicles. She pulled her body armor vest out of the trunk and donned it, fervently hoping it would be superfluous in the coming sweep. She had just finished fastening it on when Finn's car pulled in. She was relieved he'd gotten here in time and jogged over, stopping short when she saw Hugh get out of the passenger side. "Finn! What the hell is he doing here?"

"Chrissy!" Hugh grabbed her shoulders and stared into her face. "Are you all right?"

"I'm fine. Why wouldn't I be?" She threw a furious glance at her partner.

"Hugh showed up at the precinct. Neither of us could reach you and I had no idea where you were. I guess we both freaked out a bit." Finn had the grace to look somewhat shame-faced.

"Oh, for fuck's sake," she muttered and grabbed

Hugh's hand, pulling him away. She walked until she was out of earshot of her units. "Hugh, what is going on?"

"We couldn't get in touch with you! Why didn't you answer your phone?"

"Because I was putting a witness in protective custody. It was a fairly delicate situation, so I turned my phone off for a little while." She sighed as she saw him look down at his feet, kicking the gravel at the edge of the asphalt lot. "I'm sorry you were worried. Hey." She stepped closer and put her arms around him. "Work in progress?"

He hugged her as tightly as he could with her body armor in place. "Yeah, you could say that. I'm really sorry. I stopped by to bring you some flowers and see if you could go to lunch. I lost it when Finn said you were at an appointment and then we couldn't get hold of you. I thought Fiore had reneged on his promise."

"Hmm. And what did you do?"

"We went to talk to the little bastard." At the look of consternation on her face, he rushed to reassure her. "He's fine. I'm sure Finn's overreacting. Fiore won't sue; he knows he'd lose out on the hotel sale if he did."

"Oh, my God." She took his face in her hands. "This has got to stop, Hugh." He looked so forlorn and apologetic she couldn't stay mad. "Flowers, huh? What kind?"

"Roses, of course. I'm so sorry."

"Yeah, well, we'll talk about later, okay? Right now I have to go arrest some people. I need you to go sit in my car and stay there until I'm finished. I'll have a unit take you home after we get done."

"I've got a better idea. Why don't I go across the street to that coffee shop and call an Uber? I'll see you at home later if you're still speaking to me. Right now, I'll let you get back to saving the world."

He had that vulnerable look again. Her heart melted, though she knew she had every right to be furious. "Of course I'm still speaking to you. Baby steps, hon. I love you." She kissed him quickly and turned to go.

The arrests went down without a hitch; Adrian and his son were far too urbane to exhibit any sort of violence. But neither said a single word beyond asking for their lawyer. Chris knew it would be an uphill battle for the district attorney and the U.S. Attorney to make the charges stick and topple the Argyros crime family. *But I've done my part, small though it may be. I pray Ariana will find a way to be safe, both her and her baby.*

***

Finn accepted her need for secrecy with good grace, one of the many reasons they were such good partners. "If you say you couldn't tell me, I'll figure out a way to be okay with it. Sorry I couldn't control my idiot brother better."

"He's not an idiot and he's not your responsibility. Don't worry about it."

"You're not going to break up with him again, are you?" He glanced at her quickly as he drove.

She shook her head and chuckled softly. "No,

I'm in love with him and he's trying. He has a long way to go, but he's working on his attitude. This is it." She directed Finn to pull to the curb in front of a double wide trailer in the Far Horizons Mobile Home Park. An elderly woman was cleaning out a small flower bed in the minuscule front yard. The trailer was neat and tidy-looking, much like the other trailers on the street. The woman grabbed a cane lying near her and pushed to her feet.

"Hello, ma'am," Finn began, flashing his charming smile that usually worked especially well on elderly women. "I'm Detective DeLuca and this is Detective Hart. We're looking for Grady Smithson. Does he live here?"

She narrowed her eyes, taking in the badges hanging from both their necks. "I'm Mrs. Smithson. What do you want with my husband?"

"We just have a few questions for him. Is he inside?" Chris asked.

Mrs. Smithson led them up the ramp covered with green indoor/outdoor carpet. Two small Pomeranians set up a constant yapping as she pushed her way past them into a painfully neat living room. "Pel! Mel! Hush up now!" The two balls of fluff paid her no attention and continued to bark furiously as they followed her inside.

Finn caught her eye as he shook his head in disgust.

"Grady!" Mrs. Smithson hollered as she walked down the hallway, leaving Finn and Chris to wait. "There's some detectives here to talk to you."

A few minutes later, an equally elderly man hobbled out to the living room, pushing glasses on his face and buttoning a shirt as he walked. "What's this about?"

"We'd like to ask you a few questions, Mr. Smithson, about a friend of yours named George Staphros." Chris had seen the fear on the man's face as he caught sight of their badges and his wild glance toward his wife.

"Who's that?" Mrs. Smithson asked. "Grady, you don't know anyone named George Staph-whatever, do you?"

Mr. Smithson wiped a suddenly sweaty brow. "Oh, George. Well, I haven't seen him for years. Would it be possible to discuss this somewhere else, Detectives?"

"Of course, Mr. Smithson. Why don't we have our little discussion at our precinct?" Chris said.

"There's no need for that!" Mrs. Smithson barked. "You can say whatever you need to say right here."

Smithson ignored her completely. "Yes. That would be fine. I'll just get my wallet, if you don't mind." He turned to walk back to his bedroom.

"I'll go with you," Finn said firmly.

The old man deflated visibly and shuffled back to his room, Finn on his heels. Chris wondered what the crazy old coot had briefly contemplated: a shootout or a quick suicide? They returned moments later and walked quietly to the car.

"Thank you for not insisting on the handcuffs in front of my wife. She doesn't know anything."

"That's all right, Mr. Staphros. Is there anyone we can call to help take care of her? I don't imagine you'll be returning home anytime soon." Chris

247

doubted he would ever see the little trailer again; there was no statute of limitations on murder, after all. It was hard to believe this shriveled little man was responsible for the deaths of at least six people and probably dozens more. You could never tell by looking at a person.

***

It was late when she finally let herself in Hugh's house. All the questioning and accompanying paperwork had taken forever and it was past midnight when she was finally able to leave. She'd texted over an hour ago and offered to sleep at her own place that night, but he'd texted back two words:

Hugh: Come home.

She opened the door as quietly as possible, planning to slip into bed without disturbing him, but the smell of warm food greeted her, causing her empty stomach to rumble.

"Hey." Hugh appeared, wiping his hands on a dish towel. "I warmed up some soup for you. You must be starving." He ushered her back to the kitchen, where a steaming bowl of vegetable soup sat on the table next to a small plate of crackers and a glass of red wine.

She turned and threw her arms around his neck, hugging him tightly. "Thanks. This is perfect."

He hugged her back, then kissed her. "You look worn out, hon. Try to eat something and then I'll tuck you into bed next to me."

"You're spoiling me. Be careful because I could get used to this."

He smiled and pulled her chair out. "Fine by me. You deserve to be spoiled occasionally. Did everything work out all right after I left?"

She told him about the arrests while she ate the soup and sipped the wine. She explained how she had mixed emotions about arresting George Staphros. "I know he was a cold-blooded killer, but it's hard to see that in a little old man. And his wife didn't know anything about his life as a mob hitman. She honestly thought she had married Grady Smithson, a retired accountant. I hope she'll be able to recover from the shock eventually. God, that poor woman."

"What about the other wife? The one who's in protective custody? Do you think there's any chance she'll ever find a way to be safe after what she did?"

"I don't know. I hope and pray she will, but it's going to be tough." She yawned and stood to take her bowl to the dishwasher.

Hugh took it from her and placed it in the sink. "I'll get it in the morning. Let's get you to bed before you fall asleep on the table."

"Thanks for letting me come over. This wasn't much fun for you."

"Chrissy, hon." He took her face gently in his hands. "It's not always about fun. I need you with me. We belong together. It's as simple as that."

She leaned in to kiss him softly. "I love you, Hugh DeLuca."

"And I love you, Chrissy Hart. Always."

Chapter Seventeen

Three Months Later

Hugh

"Are you ready?" He paused at the door to Bella Marcone and looked at the gorgeous woman by his side.

"Are you?" she countered, eyes twinkling mischievously. "It's too late to back out, you know."

"Thank God." He opened the door for her and followed her inside. They paused at the coat check window and he helped her remove the black overcoat, revealing a short dress, somewhere between pink and ivory, with a lacy overlay. "Do you have any idea how beautiful you look tonight?"

She turned a radiant smile on him. "Why, thank you, sir. You look pretty amazing yourself. That blue tie nearly matches your eyes."

"Probably because you picked it out." He took a deep breath. "Let's do this." He led her to the back

251

of the restaurant, where their families waited for the arrival of the guests of honor. They had announced their engagement nearly three weeks ago, but had delayed an engagement party until her parents and sister could arrange to be here from El Paso. Uncle Teddy had offered to host the party, free of charge, of course.

At the door to the banquet room, she stopped and took his hand. "Hugh, the next hour or so is going to be crazy." She laughed lightly, possibly a bit hysterically. "I guess I just wanted to tell you I love you. Okay. Now I'm ready."

He grinned and kissed her before pulling open the door. Applause greeted them and he glanced around to see his entire family, several close friends, her parents and sister whom he'd met a couple times in the past months, and Father Ortega, their parish priest. He wondered if the rest of the guests were confused as to why they had invited their priest to an engagement party. He was glad to see Teddy had ensured the liquor was flowing freely; it would definitely be better if their guests weren't entirely sober. He kept Chrissy by his side as he greeted people and steadily made his way to the front of the room. "Welcome, everyone." He spoke loudly and waited for the general buzz to subside. "Thank you all for coming out to help us celebrate tonight. A few weeks ago, I asked this amazing woman to marry me." He waited for the 'awws' to die down before he continued. "And for some strange reason she said yes." He caught Chrissy's eye and winked. "Now, I know you're all under the impression that you've come here for an engagement party, but I have to disappoint you." That got everyone's attention. The room became deathly silent and Hugh saw Izzy's mouth fall open comically. "Neither of us cares much for all the fuss and stress that usually goes into a big wedding, but we did want our family and friends to be part of our big day. So, what I'm trying to say is: we're getting married tonight. Right here. This isn't an engagement party; it's our wedding." He heard a few sudden gasps—from his mother and Chrissy's, most likely—and he could swear he saw Cara mouth the words 'you little shit' to him. He took advantage of the pause to call Father Ortega up to the front of the room with them. The priest asked the guests to sit; they all obeyed, probably too shocked to do anything else, and he began the simple ceremony Hugh and Chrissy had requested.

"Before we begin, I'd like to assure those that might be worried," Father Ortega looked at Hugh's mother as he spoke, "that Hugh and Christine were married in the sight of God earlier this afternoon at Our Lady of Fatima, but they wanted to share this special ceremony with all of you."

Hugh could swear he heard his mother's sigh of relief. The preliminaries were soon over and it was time to recite the vows he'd written. "Christine Danielle Hart-DeLuca, I love you with my whole heart and soul. You are my best friend, my lover, my staunchest ally, and my toughest critic. I promise to be your greatest fan, your partner in parenthood if we are blessed with children, your accomplice in mischief, your consolation in disappointment, and your ally in conflict. This is my sacred vow to you, my love and my equal in all things."

Then it was Chrissy's turn, as soon as she wiped her eyes and could speak. "Hugh, I love you with everything I am. I take you to be my partner for life and I promise to live in truth with you and to communicate with you fully and fearlessly. I pledge to you my devotion, my love, my faith, and my honor."

They exchanged the rings they'd chosen, simple platinum bands, and Father Ortega said a prayer. Then it was time to kiss his bride. Yeah, they'd already been married for several hours and had snuck in a quick consummation after the ceremony at the church, but this felt like the real ceremony, with their families and friends surrounding them, cheering him on as he dipped her dramatically.

"If you drop me, Mr. DeLuca, you will sleep on the couch tonight with Bob."

He grinned and kissed her again. "I wouldn't dream of it, Mrs. DeLuca."

Acknowledgments

Again, I'd like to thank Agent Wayne Harvey of the New Mexico State Police for his invaluable insight into police procedurals. If I've screwed it up, the fault is mine, of course.

My amazing publishing team at Limitless is the absolute best! Thanks Lori, Elizabeth, Toni, and Deranged Doctor Designs especially.

Special thanks to my writing group, Maslow's Ding-Dongs, for their beta reads and scene critiques. Keep holding my feet to the fire!

As always, my family has my back and supports my writing career, encouraging me to keep it going, even when I doubt myself.

More than anything, I'd like to send a HUGE thanks to my readers! I love to hear from you! I write for the pure joy of storytelling, but you make the journey particularly sweet.

About the Author

Amy Reece lives in New Mexico with her incredible husband and two ridiculous mutts, Greta and Sodapop. When she's not writing, she's teaching high school English and social studies or maybe wandering through a thrift store in search of the next lucky teapot for her vast collection. She is an unrepentant bookaholic and has overflowing bookshelves in nearly every room of her house. Her favorite authors include J.R.R. Tolkien, J.K. Rowling, and C.S. Lewis–must have something to do with initials! She loves to travel and is hoping to need many research trips for future writing projects.

Did you enjoy this book? If so, please, please, please leave a short, but stellar review on amazon and/or GoodReads. I would really appreciate it!

If you want to cyber-stalk me, here are some helpful links:

Good Reads:
https://www.goodreads.com/author/show/13884337.Amy_Reece

Amazon author page:
https://www.amazon.com/Amy-Reece/e/B00WDG12RO

Facebook Fan Page:
https://www.facebook.com/areeceauthor

Twitter Fan Page:
https://twitter.com/AReeceAuthor

Website:
https://www.amyreeceauthor.com/

Blog:
https://amyreece.wordpress.com/